"Will you please leave?"

"Hey, this isn't the end of the world, you know," he said softly. "Men and women have been kissing for centuries."

"But not with total strangers," Blythe retorted. "This is certainly a first for me."

"I'm glad. I don't like to think of you in other men's arms." He caressed her chin and cupped her cheek in a tender gesture. "Since we're going to be so close, I'd better introduce myself. I'm Cad Smith."

"An appropriate name. Your parents had foresight. Don't bother to seek me out again. I have no desire to become close to you."

"You will. I don't suppose you'd care to have dinner with me tonight?" he asked hopefully.

"Hardly."

"Tomorrow, then." He grinned and closed the door softly after him.

Dear Reader:

Romance readers today have more choice among books than ever before. But with so many titles to choose from, deciding what to select becomes increasingly difficult.

At SECOND CHANCE AT LOVE we try to make that decision easy for you—by publishing romances of the highest quality every month!

Sometimes you buy romances by authors whose work you've previously read and enjoyed—which makes a lot of sense. You're being sensible . . . and careful . . . to look for satisfaction where you've found it before.

But if you're *too* careful, you risk overlooking exceptional romances by writers whose names you don't immediately recognize. These first-time authors may be the stars of tomorrow, and you won't want to miss any of their books! At SECOND CHANCE AT LOVE, many writers who were once "new" are now the most popular contributors to the line. So trying a new writer at SECOND CHANCE AT LOVE isn't really a risk at all. Every book we publish must meet our rigorous standards—whether it's by a popular "regular" or a newcomer.

This month, and in months to come, we urge you to watch for these names—Cinda Richards, Jean Fauré, Jean Barrett, and Joan Lancaster. All are dazzling new writers, an elite few whose books are destined to become "keepers." We think you'll be delighted and excited by their first books with us!

Look, too, for romances by writers with whom you're already warmly familiar: Linda Barlow, Francine Rivers, Frances Davies, and Carole Buck, among many others.

Best wishes,

Ellen Edwards

Ellen Edwards, Senior Editor
SECOND CHANCE AT LOVE
The Berkley Publishing Group
200 Madison Avenue
New York, N.Y. 10016

Second Chance at Love®

SWEET DECEPTION

DIANA MARS

SECOND CHANCE AT LOVE
BOOK

Other Second Chance at Love Books by
Diana Mars

SWEET DECEPTION

First edition published December 1984

First printing

"Second Chance at Love" and the butterfly emblem are trademarks
belonging to Jove Publications, Inc.

Printed in the United States of America

Second Chance at Love books are published by
The Berkley Publishing Group
200 Madison Avenue, New York, NY 10016

SWEET
DECEPTION

CHAPTER ONE

THE ROOM AT Indian Cove was bathed in the last sunlight of the winter day when Blythe Bedford returned from her walk. She laid her purse on the small bedside table and arched her back, suddenly aware that she no longer felt the exhaustion that had plagued her these last months. She had ignored it, as she'd ignored many things in her attempt at forgetfulness, and it had finally disappeared.

As she looked out the wide window at the snow-covered hills, Blythe said good-bye to the fatigue that had plunged her into a deep, oblivious sleep every night for almost a year now. She'd only been at the resort three days, but her long, solitary walks in the marvelously crisp Wisconsin air had done much to rejuvenate her.

She turned from the window with newfound energy. She'd never been one to feel sorry for herself, but it seemed that she had been doing quite a lot of that this year. Her husband's death had been tragic, a sad waste. But Lucas would not have approved of her surrendering to depression. She'd given her whole life to the Institute for Disabled Children these past eleven months, but she also had a duty to herself. With the crystal clarity of the icicles clinging precariously to the roof she saw that she had a life to lead. And she intended to start living it again this evening.

She pulled her white sweater over her head, intending to take a shower and change before dinner. For once, she hadn't brought a suit or a tailored dress with her. At the institute, which Lucas had founded and which she now ran herself, she wore conservative wool or cotton suits and dresses. She'd almost forgotten the feel of casual or silky clothes, and she intended to remedy that in the remaining days of her vacation.

Throwing her sweater onto the bed, she began opening the side zipper on her slacks when a key turned in the lock.

Blythe froze and watched with alarm-widened eyes as the door flew open and a giant form stepped heavily into the room. The man tossed his battered suitcase and a pair of gleaming skis on the floor just as he caught sight of her.

His golden-green eyes widened, too, but they were filled with masculine appreciation as they roved over her startled features and alighted on her flimsy lace bra. An irrepressible whistle passed his firm, wide mouth, galvanizing Blythe into action.

As she belatedly plucked her sweater from the bed and held it in front of her, Blythe also found use of her vocal cords.

"Wh-what are you doing in this room?"

The stranger held up a key that dangled from the easily recognizable tomahawk-shaped key ring of the resort.

"Hoping to discharge my belongings and take a much-needed nap," he replied. "I've been hitchhiking for two days."

Her eyes went over the tall form filling the doorway, taking in the disreputable jeans and the thick quilted jacket that was patched in several places.

A ski bum. Her brother Harlan had been one for a while. In open defiance of their parents he had brought many of his charming, carefree ski friends home with him.

A playful light shone in the stranger's remarkable golden-green eyes, and Blythe noticed with a jolt that he was handsome. The tawny hair falling rakishly over his broad forehead had been bleached by the winter sun, and his features, from the long, aristocratic nose to the square, dimpled jaw, were regular and startlingly attractive.

When he smiled, as he was doing now, two deep parallel lines were slashed into his lean cheeks, and his even white teeth shone with the glitter of a toothpaste commercial.

The fact that she found this intruder attractive unsettled her, and the way he returned her study with blatant male interest made her even more uneasy.

"Would you mind closing the door, please? I'm trying to change."

"Certainly."

He moved with a graceful alacrity for a man of his generous dimensions. Stepping over his belongings, he came farther into the room and slammed the door shut behind him.

As Blythe took an involuntary step away from him, the backs of her knees hit the edge of the bed and made her lose her balance. As she fell backward onto the bed with an exclamation of surprise, she managed to gasp, "I mean close the door *after* you. This is my room, dammit!"

The uncharacteristic swear word that escaped her lips showed her how rattled she was, and as she sat back up, Blythe tried to regain control of her shaky limbs and unsettled nerves.

The stranger's chiseled features expressed deep regret. "And here I thought you'd invited me to stay."

His eyes roamed hungrily over the creamy skin of her chest, and Blythe raised the sweater as if it were a shield.

"The only invitation I'm extending is for you to leave this room. Right now!"

He took two steps toward her, but halted in his tracks when she shrank back.

"I've been a regular since this resort opened three years ago. Since the desk clerk was called away while he was registering me, I just helped myself to a key," he explained. "Would you mind sharing a room if there are no vacancies? Obviously, fate has brought us together."

Blythe stood up and said in a low, steady voice, "No, I'm definitely *not* interested in sharing. And if you're not out of here in two seconds, I'm going to scream the place down."

The stranger shook his head sorrowfully. "Such soft blue eyes and such a hard, cold heart."

When she opened her mouth, annoyed but not afraid, and fully intending to carry out her threat, the man lunged suddenly. He clamped one hand over her mouth, and the force of his momentum caused them to tumble back onto the bed.

Blythe lay stunned for a full second, her mind a blank after the swift, unexpected attack. But she recovered quickly and began to struggle, her legs kicking and her arms flailing, her body bucking beneath the stranger's in an attempt to throw him off.

The intruder, who must have topped her five-foot-seven frame by at least six inches and sixty pounds, subdued her easily. His body covered hers, one of his hands pinned both her wrists above her head, and his legs closed around hers, trapping them easily between the muscles of his thighs.

After the intense, silent struggle, her sweater lay over her left shoulder. With her mouth and part of her nose covered by his broad, warm palm, Blythe was finding it difficult to breathe. She ceased her useless wriggling and concentrated instead on breathing in as much oxygen as she could.

The stranger seemed to sense her predicament, and he lowered one finger, which was pressing against her nostrils, to allow her an unimpeded flow of air.

Blythe became aware of the heavy and not-unpleasant weight of the hard male body blanketing hers, and the scratchy feel of his coat against the swell of her breasts. But this elemental awareness left her cold and unmoved in the face of his attack.

She could see that *he* was not unmoved. And could feel it in the slow hardening of his body on hers. A slow flush climbed his high, tanned cheekbones, and a gleam shone in his eyes as they took in the pale oval of her face and her small, straight nose offset by a slightly pointed chin that hinted at the steely determination underlying her delicate features.

Her wide blue eyes asked a silent question, which the man answered quietly.

"I'm not going to harm you. I just don't like leaving a lady's boudoir to the accompaniment of screams."

Her eyes flashed, telling him wordlessly what she thought of his remark.

The stranger smiled, that slowly unfolding grin that she knew must have been the undoing of many a susceptible female. In her present circumstances, however, she was immune.

"I don't want you to think I'm a coward who retreats in the face of the smallest opposition."

Her fury grew, but as she could not vent it orally, it emerged as a funny little gurgle in her throat.

"I know, I know," he said complacently. "You want me to release you so we can do this properly. And we will, as soon as I take a shower and make myself presentable."

Her eyes very expressively told him what she thought of that, but he continued cheerfully, "If I take my hand away, will you listen peaceably to the rest of what I have to say?"

The feral light in her narrowed gaze must have

answered him, for he continued huskily, "I guess not. But I wanted to show you that I mean you no harm. We can't afford to start off in the wrong foot, since we're going to be intimately involved. I just wanted to show you you have nothing to fear from me before I left."

He let go of her mouth suddenly, and she immediately took a large gulp of air. Then she opened her mouth to deliver the promised scream, but found her lips once more covered . . . by his mouth.

Blythe felt a sudden onset of giddiness from her recent lack of air. There was no gentle preliminary to the kiss, since her lips had already been parted when he took possession. His tongue plunged smoothly into the aperture, seeking and finding her own tongue, which he rolled with consummate seductiveness.

Blythe found herself responding blindly, her own tongue thrusting into his mouth in a burst of need. His lips, teeth, and tongue worked on her with an eroticism she hadn't previously experienced. When his tongue glided over the pearly enamel of her teeth and captured her tongue, keeping it captive in the hot cavern of his mouth, a moan broke from her throat and was consumed in their fiery kiss.

The sharp yearning sound brought her to her senses. Apalled, she realized that sometime during the kiss he'd let go of her wrists, and that her hands had moved of their own accord to his head.

She tore her mouth from his, and her fingers from the straight, silken hair, and frantically began to push at his shoulders. His lips slid over her cheek and descended to the long, smooth column of her throat.

But she pounded on his back with one hand, while with the other she grabbed a handful of his hair in an attempt to remove his mouth from her goose-bumpy flesh.

"Ouch!"

"Get off me!"

He placed a hand on his tawny head and rubbed the scalp gingerly. His passion-glazed eyes slowly regained clarity and focus, and then they locked with hers. "Stopping so soon?"

She had trouble holding his light, steady gaze. Her whole body felt on fire from the kiss, and it heated anew with shame and disgust at her behavior with a perfect stranger. "Will you please leave?" she asked shakily.

His hand went to her chin, and he held her face still as he inspected it in the rapidly decreasing light of the room.

"Hey, this isn't the end of the world, you know," he said softly. "Men and women have been kissing for centuries."

"But not with total strangers who attack them," Blythe retorted. "I don't know what kind of warped experiences you've had, but this is certainly a first for me."

"I'm glad. I don't like to think of you in other men's arms."

She looked at him, her eyes bright with tears she refused to shed. An uncontrolled trembling started deep within her body.

"Just—just go, will you? This is mortifying for me. If you were trying to prove how irresistible you are to women, you've accomplished that. Now, if you have any decency at all, please go."

"The last thing in the world I wanted was to hurt you. I'm not sure why you feel so ashamed, when I feel on top of the world at the way you responded to me. But we'll work that out later."

"There'll be no later," Blythe said, fighting the uncontrollable trembling of her body. "Please, just go."

He caressed her chin and cupped her cheek in a gesture so tender that a hot wetness once again burned in her eyes. He frowned as he looked into her tear-bright eyes.

"I don't know what's wrong yet, but I'll find out why there's so much pain and despair in those sky-blue eyes." His fingers smoothed the mauve circles under her eyes, and then he straightened up. "I'm sorry I scared you. That wasn't my intention."

He pushed himself up off the bed in an agile movement and then walked to the door. Picking up his belongings, he paused and said, "Since we're going to be so close, I'd better introduce myself. I'm Cad Smith."

Sitting up in bed, holding her sweater lightly against her chest, Blythe said dryly, "An appropriate name. Your parents had foresight." Pushing back a strand of her red hair, she added, "Don't bother to seek me out again. I have no desire to become close to you."

Incredibly, he winked at her.

"You will. I've always been good with strays, and you, Sky Eyes, are one of the sorriest sights I've seen." At the incredulous look she gave him, and

perhaps sensing her imminent retort, he hastened to
add, "Not physically, of course."

While she looked at him, torn between exasperation and amusement, he opened the door. "I don't
suppose you'd care to have dinner with me?" he asked
hopefully.

"Hardly." Now that her equilibrium was restored,
her humor had returned in full force.

"Tomorrow, then." He grinned and closed the door
softly after him.

CHAPTER TWO

THE SNOW LOOKED iridescent as Blythe set off on a snowmobile the following morning. She had risen at six after retiring early the previous night, and a good, sound sleep had done wonders for her spirits. She would have liked to deny that Cad Smith had had something to do with it, but in all honesty she couldn't. He'd unwittingly provided the impetus that set her off on the road to the recovery she'd realized she needed to make, for she could no longer remain in an emotional limbo. He had forced her to feel again.

And it had hurt.

Her anesthetized emotions had surfaced with a vengeance, and now there was no turning back. How much she'd suppressed her emotions had been evident in the hunger she had felt yesterday for the closeness and warmth of another person. She hadn't known how lonely she'd been until then. Now, finally, she could begin to let go of her past...and to build on her future.

Letting the wind whip at her face and hair, sending the red mass flying behind her, Blythe felt exhilarated. She experienced a deep communion with the mountains, snow, and white-frosted forest. The quiet and the beauty of early morning were a balm to her spirit.

But the quiet didn't last long.

She heard the whir of another machine, and with a sense of inevitability turned to see who was gaining on her. Ski goggles obscured the face, and a black ski cap covered the hair, but Blythe recognized the black-and-gray-clad body.

Cad Smith.

She tried to go faster, but her backward look cost her as she approached the crest of a gentle hill. She made an attempt to turn the snowmobile but was not able to control it in time, and she flew through the air when the vehicle came to a violent stop.

The snow cushioned her fall, and Blythe instinctively loosened her body, then curled it on impact. The force of landing knocked the breath out of her, and she felt dizzy for a while. She lay on her stomach waiting for her breath and circulation to return.

The other vehicle circled her and showered her with snow as it halted inches from her. Its occupant jumped to the ground, and she tried to lift her head as a pair of gray boots came into her line of vision, but Cad Smith's rich baritone voice barked, "Don't move! Let me check you out first."

He gently but firmly pushed her head into the snow

again while with sure, quick masculine hands he checked for broken bones. Recovered, Blythe raised her head and spit out some snow.

"At this rate, I won't leave Indian Cove alive."

She heard his deep chuckle and turned her head to glare at him. He switched from a kneeling to a sitting position next to her, and Blythe began to move cautiously.

His hand was on her back instantly, gently pressing her down as he said, "I can see you're all right, but you'd better take it easy. Give your body a chance to recover from the shock."

She heeded his advice, mostly because her knees were shaking in belated reaction. Slowly, she turned until she was lying on her side.

"I suspect you prefer women in the horizontal position," she remarked tartly.

"You're certainly right there." He leaned forward to brush the snow from her hair and flick a few drops of water from her nose, and his woodsy, elusive male fragrance drifted to her. "But I like them to be in top condition. Enjoyment should be mutual."

"I'm all right now," she said abruptly, and sat up. Her body was a little sore, but apparently functional.

He was there when she tried to get up, holding her up under the arms. When she swayed, he took her weight onto him.

"Are you sure you're okay?" he inquired solicitously.

"Never better," Blythe replied sarcastically. "I always start my winter vacations with a good spill. Things can only go uphill from there."

She pushed away from him slowly, willing all her limbs to work simultaneously as she made for her snowmobile. When Cad put a supporting arm around her waist, she didn't protest. She knew she was as uncoordinated as a newborn colt.

He righted the overturned vehicle for her and then turned back with a worried frown. "You sure you can make it back to the resort on your own steam?"

"I'm not going back," she told him, getting into the snowmobile. "I came out for a morning's sight-seeing and I intend to accomplish just that."

He sighed, obviously disliking her decision but knowing he could do nothing about it. Unsnapping his gray down vest, he said, "At least put this on. They forecast descending temperatures, and you should maintain your body heat."

Blythe was about to refuse the vest, but as he held it out for her, she decided she might as well accept it. She didn't want to become sick on her vacation. Illness would curtail her fun, and she couldn't afford to stay away from the institute for more than the week she'd allowed herself . . . not now when the institute was waiting for a decision on the grant from the Penbrook Foundation. And half of that week had already passed.

Shrugging, she said, "If you insist," and pushed her arms through the sleeve openings.

She half expected Cad to snap the front closed, but he didn't. At least he wasn't being aggressive this morning. Or, she thought as she threw him a suspicious look and spied a corner of the sensual mouth quirking upward, he was planning a more subtle offensive.

As she settled herself on the seat of the snowmobile again, he took off his ski cap and pulled it down over her flaming tresses.

"Mmmm. Black looks good on you."

She ignored his compliment, raising her hand to take off the cap. His hand was there to stay her.

"But your head," she protested. "Without your vest and hat, you can catch a cold."

"Then you'll have to nurse me, won't you?" Grinning, he mounted his own orange and black vehicle.

She shook her head, but left the hat in place. His hair was slicked back from his wide forehead by the wind, and the sun picked up gold glints in it as well as silver glints from the lenses of his goggles. She couldn't help noticing how truly handsome he was. But his pure physical beauty did not affect her as viscerally as it had yesterday when he'd caught her at a raw, low moment. She'd been ashamed of her behavior then, but in the cool light of morning she'd realized it had been more than a sexual response. It had also been a reaching out for another human being, an affirmation of life. Lucas was gone, and she would always miss him, but life was meant to be lived, not merely survived. She'd been able to forgive herself for what she'd seen as a betrayal of Lucas's memory when she'd realized that she had to let him go.

Cad's words cut through her reverie, and she realized she'd been staring at him as though in a trance.

"Have you changed your mind about sight-seeing? Would you like to come back to the hotel for a cup of hot chocolate?"

She shook her head again, exasperated by his persistence but reluctantly charmed by his cheerful, admiring air. It had been a long time since she'd basked in the glow of a man's appreciation, and she was enjoying the sensation.

"Thank you, but no. Hot chocolate has a way of burning the unwary."

"I make the best hot chocolate this side of the lake," he claimed. "Sure you don't want to give it a try?"

She smiled. "No, thanks. I'd rather stay away from temptation altogether. Of any kind." Pulling on the black cap more securely, she told him, "Thanks for the loan. I'll return your cap and vest as soon as I get back."

She set off without waiting for his answer and told herself to be wary. Cad Smith might be an itinerant ski bum, but he possessed a lively intelligence. He would be fine for a mild flirtation, but she wasn't ready for a heady involvement at this stage in her life.

During the next hour as she skirted hilltop lookouts, a river gorge, converted railroad trestles, and an ice volcano, Blythe saw why Indian Cove was rapidly becoming so well known. She'd been lucky to come before it expanded to the mammoth size of the Colorado or German resorts.

Now she was feasting her eyes on an enchanting sight that reminded her of a magical snow scene in a movie she'd seen long ago. The forest was blanketed in white, with delicate icicles hanging from the branches of the trees. And in the middle of the sculpted ice and evergreen beauty, a waterfall appeared, taking her breath away. Blythe cut the engine, climbed off the snowmobile, and stood at the edge of the half-frozen river, shivering from the actual cold emanating from the ice-encrusted falls as well as from the sight of the glacial scene before her.

She was grateful now that Cad had given her his vest. It didn't particularly match her vivid aqua and white suit, but its thick padding was certainly welcome. So was the wonderful feel of his wool cap over her cold ears.

For a long moment, Blythe stood still in front of the waterfall, studying the way the water cascaded in a silver curtain, shimmering like millions of diamonds under the pale winter sun.

So lost was she in her awed contemplation that she didn't hear steps crunching in the snow until they were upon her.

She turned with swift fear, suddenly realizing that she was all alone in an isolated, wildly primitive spot. But her heartbeat diminished to a low roar and her frantic pulse subsided as she saw who had approached her.

"You startled me," she told him in a cool tone. Why had he followed her?

"Sorry. I just wanted to make sure you were all right."

"Pangs of a guilty conscience hitting you belatedly?"

He grinned. "No guilt. I will admit that my timing might have been a bit off yesterday, but that's because you're keeping up some sort of barrier between us."

"How convenient to blame the woman, to pretend that I'm playing some sort of game. And how smug."

"That's not what I said. I'm not blaming you. Nor

am I taking you for granted. But you must admit that it was instant combustion between us."

She turned her head and looked him straight in the eye. "Combustion had nothing to do with it, Mr. Smith. You simply caught me at an unguarded moment, that's all."

His grin was crooked. "Then I'll just have to engineer another . . . unguarded moment."

Her blue eyes frosted over. "I wouldn't advise pouncing on me again, Mr. Smith. I didn't much appreciate being scared half out of my wits."

His expression sobered. "I apologize for alarming you. But it would have been embarrassing if you'd screamed."

"Not for me. Do you make a habit of invading women's rooms?"

"Not till now, no. Women usually await my arrival with a bottle of champagne and open arms."

Her eyes flashed at his outrageous boast.

"I recommend assertiveness training for you," she told him ironically. "Seems to me you have a rather poor self-image. That's why you're so shy and insecure." He walked over to her and put an arm around her shoulders as she went on, "And what occupies your time when you're not being welcomed in ladies' boudoirs?"

"The situation rarely arises."

She gazed thoughtfully up at him. Though she didn't doubt his persuasive charm with women, she was sure there was more to his life than a series of romantic escapades. Cad Smith was certainly making himself appear insouciant and totally unambitious, and yet she felt it was an act. After all, even ski bums had a sense of purpose in their lives, even if it was only the next run, the next slalom, the next downhill, that they directed their ambition toward. They arranged their lives, their schedules, and even their work around the search for the big thrill.

Probing, she said casually, "So you just ski and . . ."

"Definitely *and*."

Her eyes roved over him. "For a ski bum, you're certainly well dressed today."

"Tools of the trade." His left hand trapped an errant strand of red hair and tucked it beneath the cap, and Blythe realized he must be ambidextrous. Or close to it. "Even ski bums have to work to support their passion." He paused and eyed her hungrily. "Or passions."

Uneasy and skeptical, she took his hand and lowered it to his side. "I'm cold. I'd like to go back now."

To his credit, he didn't say the obvious. She'd been right in suspecting that Cad's methods were far too subtle for that.

"Hungry?" he asked her as they made their way to the snowmobiles.

"Now that you mention, it, yes. Ravenous."

"Care to have breakfast with me?"

She looked at him askance as she mounted her own red and black vehicle.

"I promise to be on my best behavior," he continued. "Besides, what could I do in a crowded, family-style restaurant?"

"A man who's used to being greeted with open arms and bottles of champagne? I'm sure you'd think

of something," she told him wryly as she revved the
engine of her snowmobile.

"Thank you for your confidence. It warms the cock-
les of my heart."

"As long as that's all that's warmed," she told him,
taking a quick view of the waterfall and imprinting in
her mind its timeless, untamed beauty. Once back in
the city, she'd need memories of the freedom and
lightheartedness of this morning.

She sent the snowmobile plunging through the
frosty, clean-smelling snow, and Cad followed. Over
the whine of the two engines, he yelled, "Will you
spend the morning with me? Yes or no?"

She extended the engine, trying to outdistance him,
but he kept up with her. She hesitated, debating the
pros and cons of spending the morning with him. She
was wary of any deep involvement, but she did want
to rejoin the land of the living. She enjoyed Cad's
company and witty repartee. As the intoxication of
speed and wind whipped around her, and the vibration
of the engine surged through, she asked herself, with
impulsive optimism, What harm could it do?

Knowing she could not outrace him, she yelled
into the snow-scented breezes, "All right. Breakfast
it is," and swerved sharply to head toward the cav-
alcade of snowmobiles dotting the road back to the
lodge, which they were fast approaching.

Cad waved as he went past her, and Blythe in turn
waved to a fellow snowmobiler, who let her in ahead
of him. Apparently, others had wanted to take ad-
vantage of the incomparable peace and loveliness of
a fresh winter morning.

She smiled as she recognized that joining the group on impulse had been a symbolic way of rejoining the human race. In her anger and hurt over her husband's death, she'd turned away from other people, and now was glad to be welcomed back into the fold.

Smiling more wholeheartedly than she'd done in the past year, Blythe entered the lodge in search of Cad.

CHAPTER THREE

Just as she spotted Cad at a table on the sun deck, a desk clerk approached her.

"Mrs. Bedford? You had an urgent telephone message from a Mr. Justin Harris. He asked that you call him back as soon as possible."

Blythe looked at Cad once more, his back silhouetted against the snow-covered slopes, and sighed.

"Thank you. I'll make the call now."

As she followed the clerk to the phone, she wondered why Justin had called her at the resort. It was mostly at his instigation that she'd taken a brief vacation. And she'd done so only because she knew that Justin, her assistant at the institute, could ably cover for her until she returned. A lawyer as well as a CPA, Justin was truly overqualified for his own position, and Blythe had complete confidence in his ability to meet any challenges and manage any crises that might occur in her absence.

Justin's voice was brittle when he answered her call on the first ring.

"Blythe, they turned down our request for the grant. That damn Penbrook Foundation refused to even consider funding the innovations that you outlined in your report."

She tried to keep her voice calm despite the bitterness that assailed her. "Did you talk to Vincent Nimms?"

"Sure. I spoke to him, and he said if you have anything to add to your proposal, you should do it personally. He was used to dealing with Lucas, and he says he doesn't work with delegates. Not that he's about to change his mind for you, either. That old bastard—"

"Justin, take it easy. You know Vincent hates women, children, and dogs on principle. And not necessarily in that order. How he ever got that job I'll never know..." Then, realizing she was letting herself get carried away, she added in her usual brisk tone, "I'll come back right away. I'll go to Vincent myself and make the old curmudgeon see reason."

"You'll take the three days you've still got coming, Blythe," Justin said in an unusual display of authority. She could just picture him—businesslike in his impeccable three-piece suit, his brown hair receding prematurely, those astute, brown eyes looking deceptively bland behind his glasses. He could have a job anywhere he desired, but he was content to remain with her. Because of Lucas. "I told Nimms you were away on an urgent personal matter, and he made an appointment for you to see him next Wednesday. Generous old buzzard."

"Thanks, Justin. I'm not sure I'll take all three days, but I will stay here today at least. This might be my last chance to get away for a while."

"I think you should stay the entire week," Justin began stubbornly.

"I appreciate that, Justin," Blythe cut in, warmed by his concern. Justin had been a good friend of her husband's ever since their high school days, and when Lucas had died, Justin had been there for her to lean on. He'd seen her through her disbelief, grief, and finally, mourning. But she was ready to stand alone now. "Tell me, though, did Nimms offer you any specific criticism of my grant proposal or just a general rejection of it?"

"Yes, he did criticize two or three of your ideas in detail." Justin recounted the phone conversation to her and added, "But he didn't offer much hope. I think the creep enjoys making people squirm."

Blythe couldn't help smiling at this sadly accurate picture of Vincent Nimms. She'd tried to respect his advanced age—since she could respect nothing else about the man—in her dealings with him, but it was true that his thin, dour visage lightened up only when he was able to categorically refuse something.

"I'll let some ideas germinate in my mind. Who knows? Maybe I can come up with a way to work around his objections," she said optimistically. Justin was a whiz at math and computers, but Blythe had always been the idea person at the institute. Her creative brain liked to look at pieces of a puzzle and put them together in an entirely new and more productive whole.

With some final words of reassurance to Justin, Blythe ended their conversation. By the time she returned to the sun deck, she wasn't sure Cad would still be there.

He was.

She approached with a sunny smile, shelving her problems until she could deal with them in private. She saw that Cad was finishing his breakfast, and as he held the chair out for her, she also noticed that his golden-green eyes lacked their usual warmth.

"Took you a good half-hour to decide whether you'd grace the table of a poor ski bum?" he greeted her ungraciously.

His soft, sarcastic attack caught her unaware. She'd become used to his casual charm, and this serious, embittered tone surprised her.

"I'm sorry I'm late, but my assistant called, and I couldn't—"

"You work?" She suddenly hated this new side of Cad Smith. He lifted one eyebrow superciliously as he said, "Of course. You do charity work, right? Or do you run an expensive boutique on an exclusive street?" He hooked one arm over the back of his chair as he regarded her skeptically. "I wonder if you'd have left one of your dates cooling his heels for thirty minutes." At her puzzled frown, he added, "Although it probably wouldn't have mattered to you, would it?"

"What do you mean by that crack?" Blythe was

slow to anger, but once the fuse was lit, the explosion could be earth-shaking.

"I mean that rich girls think they have the world in their hands and men by their tails."

"That's a very negative generalization," she said, her anger simmering and rapidly reaching a boil. "And what makes you think I'm rich?"

"Your poise, your bearing, your accent, your speech patterns. Not to mention the expensive gold bracelet you're wearing."

She instinctively touched the bracelet, a present from her parents on her eighteenth birthday. That was one of the things she'd kept when she'd left home to marry Lucas. Her parents had disowned her, and she had taken the piece of jewelry in case she and Lucas were ever in desperate need of cash. Soon, they had been desperate—not for themselves, but for one of the institute's children in an emergency, and Blythe had pawned the bracelet. On the second anniversary of their marriage, Lucas's gift to her had been to redeem the bracelet from the pawnshop.

A waiter came over, cutting into her painful thoughts, and Blythe waved him away. Her appetite had deserted her.

"I was ready to overlook your boorish behavior of yesterday, Mr. Smith," she told Cad, "but this is too much. I hate snobs—even inverted ones. And I work for a living—out of necessity, not boredom."

She pushed her chair back, not caring that its noisy scrape on the wooden deck attracted the attention of several patrons. "I've lost my appetite, Mr. Smith. I suggest you keep away from now on. I don't need *your* hang-ups on *my* vacation."

Turning on her booted heel, she walked away, rigid with fury that he had mistaken her for precisely the kind of person she despised so much! How her mother, the inimitable and redoubtable Penelope Bedford, would have enjoyed witnessing the scene that had just transpired on the sun deck. And her father, the venerable Baldwin Bedford, would have clapped Cad on the back and exclaimed, "That's the way, boy. You've got to show a woman who's boss," conveniently ignoring the fact that he'd relinquished the reins to his iron-willed wife on innumerable occasions.

As she neared the beautifully polished mahogany stairs, Blythe realized she hadn't felt such a glorious rush of emotion in a long time—except for yesterday when Cad had scratched away the veneer of her defenses. She reflected that Cad was capable of eliciting many emotions from her. The chief one being anger.

But what he'd said was unforgivable. How dare he categorize her as a frivolous, self-indulgent post-deb, when she was nothing of the kind! It was only as she began taking the steps two at a time in a hurried, furious flight to her bedroom that she realized Cad held many of her own views about rich people. Only his objections seemed to have centered on rich women—and that had stung. Blythe was painfully aware how many of her girlhood friends had chosen exactly the sort of lifestyle that Cad had ridiculed.

Still, she told herself as she opened the door to her room and closed it behind her with a resounding slam, Cad's comments had been unjust. After all, he'd known her well enough to form an opinion of her character, even if their acquaintance was less than twenty-four hours old.

He should have given her the benefit of the doubt. He ought to have let her explain. The fact that he hadn't only meant that her first impression had been right: He was better lost than found.

He'd better keep away from her from now on.

Cad *did* keep away from her, at least for the remainder of the day. Blythe was thankful that she didn't see him when she went down for lunch after a long, therapeutic shower.

She ate a substantial lunch. The pure mountain air had revived her appetite, and skipping breakfast had made her ravenous. She went skiing in the afternoon and thought she spied Cad's tall form on the slalom slope, but she didn't bother to confirm the impression. Her temper was still at the boiling point.

That evening there was to be a wine and cheese party for the guests at Indian Cove Ski Resort. Blythe loved cheese fondue, and not even the prospect of meeting Cad there dimmed her anticipation of the event.

She dressed carefully in midnight-blue velvet slacks and a matching top, liking the sensual feel of the material on her skin. She put her hair up in an intricate twist and added her gold bracelet as the final touch.

Looking in the mirror, Blythe was satisfied with her appearance. She'd lost the unnatural pallor she'd sported when she'd first arrived at Indian Cove, and the dark circles beneath her eyes were almost completely gone.

Grabbing a clutch purse, she tightened the ankle straps on her sling-back sandals and walked over to the dresser to retrieve her key.

She left the room in a barely perceptible cloud of violet fragrance, and her step quickened as she neared the source of the happy din.

The party was in full swing when she arrived. Most of the guests had congregated around the fondue table and were freely imbibing of the white wine.

As she moved forward into the gregarious group, edging closer to the giant fireplace that dominated one wall of the lounge, a glass appeared in her line of vision. Blythe raised her hand automatically, thinking it was being proffered by one of the waiters who were circulating among the crowd. But she stepped back instinctively when she saw who was holding the glass.

Running her hand along her velvet-covered flank in a nervous gesture, Blythe absently registered that Cad looked striking in a dark brown suit and lime-green turtleneck, his tawny hair combed into a semblance of order.

The glow from the fireplace seemed to mold his features, emphasizing the strong planes and hollows of his face and the serious expression in his light eyes. His voice vibrated toward her in a rich, deep tone that somehow managed to carry over the laughter and conversations all around them.

"We have to talk," he said. His voice indicated that he wouldn't take no for an answer.

CHAPTER FOUR

BLYTHE WASN'T ABOUT to let him intimidate her. She met his gaze coolly and said, "I think not," then turned and walked away.

But Cad was apparently not easily discouraged. He casually followed her and remained at her side.

Furious, Blythe thought of leaving the party. But why should she allow this odious man to dissuade her from enjoying the party that she'd looked forward to all day? It was he who had been unfair, unreasonable . . . and undaunted.

Going off into a quiet corner of the room—certain he'd follow—she confronted him and told him so.

"I plead guilty," he told her with a slow smile that threatened to melt her to the soft consistency of the delicious cheese she was eating. Angry at her weakness, she dipped a crispy piece of toast into the cheese, which almost spilled over the side of her dish, and glared alternately at the cheese and Cad.

"Then why don't you get—" The word *lost* stuck in her throat—oh, those etiquette lessons of her youth that still inhibited her at every turn! "Why not get more wine and drown your remorse?" she finished eventually.

Cad leaned toward her, bracing her arm across her only avenue of escape, trapped as she was against the wall, and murmured, "Because I won't sleep tonight if I can't apologize. My behavior on the sun deck was atrocious."

"I'll say," Blythe agreed, her eyes seeking an avenue of escape as she ostensibly took delicate sips of the exquisite wine.

"And whether you're rich or not is none of my business. The fact that I've had a bad experience—" He cut himself off, and Blythe looked at him suspiciously. Did he really think her dense enough to swallow some heartbreaking account of an affair with a wealthy girl? If there had been such an affair, it was probably ruined because of all those other women ardently welcoming him with champagne. She knew how fascinating ski bums were. And this one bum whose enticing body was a suffocating inch away from her was the *crème de la crème*.

Smiling engagingly, he added, "I really think we had something going. And I'd hate to see us lose it because of the oversized chip on my shoulder. Whether you work or not is immaterial..." Seeing her blue eyes whip into a seastorm, he raised a palm and added placatingly, "Though I believe that you *do* work."

"Thank you for your big vote of confidence," she interjected dryly.

"But regardless of what happened earlier," he continued, "I would like us to take up where we left off."

Blythe's blue eyes narrowed, and she asked silkily, "You mean half-naked on the bed, where you threw me down and forced yourself on me?"

"Where you tried to scream and I prevented you," he reminded her gently. "After that, things happened spontaneously."

She put her left hand on his arm, and felt its rock-hard solidity underneath her touch. She pushed. He didn't budge.

She looked longingly at the crowd of people only a few feet away, all happily partaking of the feast. Her eyes followed the path of a waiter who weaved skillfully in and out of the crowd. And she let her hand drop in defeat. The social protocol she had grown up with was still deeply ingrained in her: She could not call out for assistance and risk making a scene.

"Would you search deep within you and try to find some vestiges of civility, Mr. Smith, and let me pass? Even you must have been taught better manners by your mother."

"But I'm a lowly orphan, who was shunted from place to place, family to family."

She looked him steadily in the eye, keeping her gaze above the too appealing line of his sensual mouth.

"Let's not kid around. You're no more an orphan than I am. I, too, recognize education and a certain speech pattern when I hear it, Mr. Smith." She lowered her eyes pointedly to his arm, and repeated, "Please let me pass."

He stepped aside, saying, "Ask and ye shall receive."

As she passed by him, she muttered, "Ye be careful of what ye may receive one of these moons."

His rich, seductive laugh trailed after her when she approached the table to secure some more fondue and a few of the raw vegetables—celery, carrot sticks, green pepper—that were arranged festively on silver platters.

Determined to avoid Cad Smith for the remainder of the evening, she joined a small group at the end of one of the food-laden tables strategically arranged in a hexagon. As she approached, she heard a portly man protest, "Frances, you know raw vegetables are bad for my ulcer. It's all I can do to stumble into my office every morning and remain there for the rest of the day."

The woman beside him—evidently Frances— sniffed, and said, "Nelson dear, the operative word is *stumble*. And if your ulcer's so bad, how come you're not curtailing your intake of other substances— liquid, if you know what I mean?"

Blythe was about to edge away from this group, which reminded her of many she'd encountered at the Caldwell Country Club back home, but found her polite exit blocked when she bumped into a granite wall.

The granite wall suddenly sprouted rocklike extensions that closed about her hip as she tried to move sideways. She didn't need to be told whom she'd bumped into—her body had already reacted to stimuli and transmitted them lightning-quick to the rest of her stiffened body.

"I'm sure Nelson dutifully ingests a gallon of milk a day, don't you, Nels, old sport?" Cad remarked lightly.

Frances shot visual daggers at Cad, which he withstood imperturbably, his grin fully in place. Nelson harrumphed, and said, "Well, yes, of course, old fellow . . . Say, what is your name? Don't recall meeting you here before . . ."

"Cad Smith." Cad extended his right hand, but kept his left firmly in place as he brought Blythe more fully against his loins. "I come here every year, but we must have missed each other."

"That wouldn't be hard," a handsome black-haired man, obviously in Nelson's party, said. His interested eyes roved over Blythe, and she fumed inwardly at Cad's show of possessiveness. Oh, for freedom from those iron-clad conventions imposed on her since the cradle. "Considering this is your first time here, Nelson."

Frances laughed, intending to fill the awkward silence, but the shrill sound vibrated uncomfortably through the group. Still trying to smooth things over, she asked, "I assume you're here for the skiing, Mr. Smith?"

Blythe looked up at Cad, almost dreading the answer he'd give. She'd already felt the spasm of amusement that had traveled from his body to hers at the woman's pompousness.

She closed her eyes as he winked. "Among other things, Mrs. . . ."

"Carpenter," the woman supplied.

"Carpenter. I like to do a little fishing, too," he confided conspiratorially.

"In midwinter?" Frances's voice carried the chill of the season in it.

"Certainly. That's the best catch of the season, when everything lies dormant, ready to be awakened and rejuvenated."

Blythe opened her eyes to find herself staring right into the amused gaze of the dark-haired man. She blushed—another first in a long time—and surreptitiously tried to remove Cad's hands from her hips. They merely tightened tenaciously.

"Yes, you see, I have this theory," Cad continued. "I figure both fish and women go through seasonal changes, and I make my moves accordingly." He winked again, and said, "That way I have a woman to clean and cook the fish, and attend to my needs after the fishing and eating are done."

Frances turned a lovely shade of purple, to match her gown. "Mr. Smith." Her scandalized tone reminded Blythe of what she'd left behind—a world of hypocrisy that condemned the failings and shortcomings of the masses, but indulged in its own peccadilloes left and right. The trick was not to get caught—and never, never to be flagrant or obvious about it. That was the ultimate sin.

"Mr. Smith," Frances intoned righteously again, lifting thin shoulders on which her dress hung like crochet work on a hanger, despite its exclusive styling. "You need a lesson in manners." Her brown eyes went to Cad's hands, and she added, "I just don't know how that lovely woman puts up with you."

Before Cad could say something outrageous again, Blythe anticipated him. Grinding the high heel of her shoe into his instep and digging her nails into his hand, she ignored his pained gasp and stepped away.

"You'll have to excuse poor Cad. He confided in me today what an awful time he had in orphanages when he was growing up. Lack of love, you know. Stunts one's growth." When three pairs of eyes convened on Cad's larger-than-life dimensions, she added hurriedly, "One's emotional growth, that is. He's a toucher. And he can't bear to be alone for more than a few minutes."

Turning to avoid the skepticism, amusement, and bafflement she saw in the three surrounding gazes, she patted Cad's cheek softly and said, "You'll be okay, Cad. There are lots of lovely ladies here who'll be happy to clean fish for an orphaned ski bum." To the others, she said, "It's been a pleasure. If you'll excuse me, I'm going to try some dessert now."

As she moved away, she saw Cad gingerly move his foot. She knew her spike heel must have left quite an impression, but he had asked for it. Lord knew what he would have said had she allowed him to continue. It was obvious he took a perverse pleasure in shocking people.

She wasn't alone for long. As she was helping herself to brandied fruit compote and Black Forest cake, she was joined by the dark-haired man who'd been standing with the Carpenters.

"Known Mr. Smith for long?" he asked her.

"Seems an eternity," she answered as she poured herself a glass of ice water. She'd already had three glasses of wine, and her level of gaiety was just about right.

"Will you be staying long?" he went on. Blythe gave him a questioning glance, and he said, "I'm sorry. Let me introduce myself." He extended a long, narrow, well-manicured hand. "My name's Stan Martin."

Blythe smiled and shook hands. "Blythe Bedford. I'm not yet sure how long I'll remain here. Possibly only till tomorrow."

"Now that would be a pity." He picked up a black olive and chewed on it thoughtfully. "Can't you possibly extend your stay? I'll be here another forty-eight hours."

Blythe shook her head. "I don't think so. I have to get back to work. This was really not the time for me to go away, but I felt—"

"As if you needed to rejuvenate yourself?"

She laughed. "Yes, but not the way 'wild Cad Smith' implied."

"Well, if you're not...attached to wild Cad, would you consider spending tomorrow with me?"

An arm went about Blythe's waist before she could reply. "No, I'm afraid not, buddy," Cad answered for her. His tone was lazy, his body rigid. "She's spending tomorrow with me."

Stan stiffened. "I think the lady should have something to say about that."

Cad looked down into her eyes and said softly, "The lady knows what her answer will be."

Blythe looked from one to the other. Stan was the shorter and slimmer of the two. But it wasn't only his build that told Blythe he would be the loser in a physical fight, just as it wasn't only the fear of causing a scene that had made Blythe put a stop to the quickly escalating antagonism.

Cad was the more determined of the two; he was the craftier, stronger, and wilier. Blythe knew that his lazy, carefree pose hid an iron will. And she didn't want to see Stan humiliated, nor did she want to be fought over like a bone claimed simultaneously by two dogs.

"Gentlemen." She had to repeat the word. Both men were lost in a male world of weighing up and psyching out. She spoke louder to prevent the imminent confrontation. "Gentlemen, you seem to have forgotten one thing." Now she had both men's attention. "Me. I am not flattered by your willingness to fight over me, since you've seen fit to overlook my own preference."

"And that is?" Cad encouraged softly, obviously confident of her reply.

Blythe looked at him incredulously. The man's confidence was unshakable.

She smiled sweetly. "A good book. *War and Peace*." Taking one last bite of dessert, she set her plate down. "I suggest you gentlemen concentrate on the latter subject of the book. Good night."

Stan took an involuntary step toward her, as if to stop her, while Cad's face broke into that wide, unfolding grin. Damn, but he was attractive!

Ignoring the little leap her heart gave in its confining cavity, she took a couple of tart apples from the table and made her way upstairs. Her hand caressed the rich mahogany banister as she regally climbed the steps.

All through the nightly ritual of showering and changing into a nightgown, Blythe worried about Vincent Nimms, in whose skeletal, stingy fingers her grant proposal resided. Although she knew that as soon as she got back she'd be creatively juggling the figures again, she was afraid Vincent might have already decided that his rejection was final. Perhaps he was just seeking a delay to make it seem as though he'd studied every angle and done his best for the institute.

His rejection of her proposal was doubly aggravating because Blythe had economized wherever possible. She had learned to live frugally during her marriage to Lucas, and had never thirsted for money in any case. Unlike many people from her old circle, Blythe had always seen money as a means to an end, not as an end in itself. She didn't understand people whose aim was to amass more money than they'd ever need in the search for status, power, and that most elusive ingredient of all, happiness.

But Blythe knew how fleeting *that* commodity was. Since Lucas's death, she had come to be content with satisfaction in her work. The institute gave shape and purpose to her life, and the children meant the world to her.

She realized, however, that this vacation had accomplished one thing: It had shown her how out of touch with people she'd become. Even though she hadn't found much in common with the guests she'd met, she'd enjoyed the trivial social discourse. It represented human contact, and there'd been precious little of that since Lucas died. Her social life had dwindled as she buried herself in work, and many of her friends had begun to get offended when she continued to turn down their kind invitations to dinner or get-togethers.

Full of renewed optimism, she resolved to remedy that on her return home. Then, with uncharacteristic impulsiveness, she began to change again from her nightgown into a pair of slacks and a sweater.

The thought of the roaring fire downstairs had been haunting her, and she knew she could no longer resist its lure. As she pulled on a pair of loafers, she hoped she wouldn't meet Cad down there. But she dismissed the possibility. After all, it had been well over two hours since she'd left the party. Surely it had ended by now.

The prospect of curling up by the fire in splendid isolation while she planned her future suddenly seemed much more appealing to Blythe than getting into bed. Taking her book and an apple, she quickly and silently made her way downstairs.

Everyone had left the lounge, and the staff had made quick work of the cleanup.

The room was in shadows, bathed only in an orange-blue light that beckoned her with hypnotic strength. A nice, roaring fire after a hard, challenging day on the slopes had always been one of the attractions of ski resorts for Blythe.

Bringing a huge, comfortable chair closer to the welcoming fire, she snuggled in its velvet softness.

It was big enough so that she could curl her legs underneath her, and she took off her loafers, set the book on her lap, and began munching on her apple. She stared into the flames that leaped, danced, and hid behind the logs in an acrobatic, incendiary ballet.

Blythe sighed as she remembered that Lucas had not liked to ski—had in fact disliked any type of athletic activity—and with him she had missed the companionable sharing of the peaceful exhaustion that hard exercise and pushing oneself to the limit could bring. Oh, well. With another sigh, Blythe gave in to the mesmerizing and noisy performance of the fire, her ears finely attuned to and seduced by the crackle, pop, and fizz of logs burnt and resettled, their familiarity soothing...

She started when a deep voice rumbled, "May I join you?" Cad Smith had found her once again.

CHAPTER FIVE

HIS BARITONE VOICE inches from her ear had Blythe jumping in her chair, her half-eaten apple rolling across the floor. Crossly, she looked up into guarded golden-green eyes that were doing their best to confuse, conquer, and ultimately seduce her.

Cad bent in one open smooth motion and retrieved her apple. Blythe noticed that he wore the same clothes he'd had on when she took her aggravated leave of him, minus the jacket. The wool of the turtleneck stretched across his broad shoulders when he stooped, and smoothed out on his well-delineated muscles when he straightened.

As Cad tossed the apple into the enormous fireplace, she said, "Mr. Smith. I've come here to be alone."

He turned to face her, his skin golden in the wavering reflection from the fire.

"Come now. No more of this Mr. Smith stuff," he chided her softly. "Not after all our intimacy."

"Intimacy?" she questioned dangerously.

"Sure. It's not every day I have a hole drilled through my foot. I'm considering suing you for disabling me."

Her eyes traveled the length of his long, muscular legs. "I didn't notice a limp."

He leaned forward. "That's because I'm good at hiding my afflictions. But you were right, my emotional growth was stunted by a lack of love. Would you care to remedy the situation?"

She pushed at the chest so marvelously defined by his clinging sweater and said pointedly, "I came here in search of some quiet solitude."

Cad went down on his haunches next to her, his eyes only inches above hers. "I don't believe that. I was here first, so it follows that you were seeking me out."

Blythe laughed, a sound filled with incredulity and exasperation. Cad pointed to another chair in the shadows, which she'd only peripherally registered when she came into the room. "I was sitting right there."

"Hiding?" she asked caustically. "Most people like to sit near a fire."

"I don't have to. I'm hot enough."

Truly angry now, Blythe got to her feet, her fingers closing about her leather-bound book.

But Cad pushed her gently down.

"Please, stay. I didn't mean to chase a guest out of my—" Pausing, he rose and added, "This is certainly not my private domain. I saw you come in, and I meant to leave you to your thoughts, but you proved too irresistible. I promise I won't irritate you any further. I'll just fade into the woodwork."

Blythe subsided uncertainly. She had to admit that she found his attentions flattering. And she didn't fear him. She even experienced a certain exhilaration in his presence.

But she had come here to read and meditate and gather about her a mantle of mental resources. That certainly would not be possible with this disturbing man sitting only inches away from her.

On the other hand, she was a paying guest at the ski lodge. Why should she let him drive her away? And why should she allow him to exert any influence on her coming and goings? She would stay, if only for a short while, she decided, satisfied with her masterful rationalization.

But after a few restless, fidgety minutes in which she could concentrate neither on her book nor on her meditation, she glanced in his direction.

Cad was quietly, lazily sprawled on his chair. True to his word, he'd retreated and had remained out of her direct line of vision. He seemed lost in his own thoughts, his body expressing a degree of relaxation that she could not seem to attain, his folded hands resting in his lap.

Feeling an unwanted, uncomfortable rush of heat travel over her skin with prickly intensity, Blythe took her eyes off Cad's long-fingered hands and trim, taut midsection.

"Do you have to lurk in the shadows?" she asked

suddenly, unaware that she was going to ask the question and surprised at her own perversity.

But Cad had no trouble with her request. "Certainly not. If I'm disturbing you here, I'll move closer to the fire."

He did exactly that. With athletic grace, he stretched out on the rug in front of the hearth, and Blythe soon found herself completely distracted from all thoughts of work, taking silent pleasure in the sight of the large, muscular form on which the flames drew colorful pictures.

Dragging her eyes away from the red-gold halo of his hair, she said the first thing that came to her mind. "I just thought of something else I like about this unusual resort. There's no moosehead on the wall, an unfortunate tradition in many other resorts. I, for one, can do without that kind of hallmark."

Cad lay on his side and looked up at her. "The owner prefers to decorate the walls with artwork done by the Indians of Wisconsin."

"Oh?" Blythe considered this bit of information. "Do you know the owner?"

"We're intimate friends," Cad said, his smile roguish. "Why do you think I find a place to stay here every year?"

"Is the owner a woman?" Blythe asked. "If so, there was no need for you to try to persuade me to share a room with you."

"The owner is a man. And no other room in this place contains anything as special as you. I enjoy all of the amenities."

Blythe shifted in her seat, half-annoyed, half-amused.

"I don't like hearing myself described as an amenity."

"But you're not. You're a warm, passionate woman who has a kind enough heart to forgive my transgressions."

Blythe laughed, enjoying their verbal sparring. Many things Cad Smith might be; dull was not one of them.

"You *are* clever. That means if I don't forgive your future transgressions, I'll be coldhearted."

His eyes bore into hers. "Never."

Lost in his gaze, Blythe did not realize her whole body had gone lax until her book dropped from boneless fingers. Cad stretched forward to pick it up for her, then retreated, upholding his promise to keep his distance.

With surprising tact, he went on to cover many trivial topics, deftly deflecting the pointed questions about himself that Blythe posed. When she had begun to relax once more, lulled into the false security offered by pleasant conversation, a crackling fire, and the nocturnal silence all around them, Cad asked, "Why are you hurting?"

Surprised, Blythe stared at him silently.

Cad added softly, "You look a hell of a lot better than you did the first time I saw you. But there's still a haunting sadness in your face, Sky Eyes. What are you trying to forget?"

A painful smile broke through Blythe's restrained expression. She hadn't discussed Lucas's death, or the guilt that had followed, with anyone except Justin, and only once with him. Justin had seen her through the many moods that had finally mellowed into acceptance, but his had been a silent support. She hadn't allowed anything else. She'd been afraid she'd disintegrate if she allowed anyone too close to her pain.

"We all have painful things in our past, Mr. Smith. That's part of life."

"But someone as young as you shouldn't have to carry the world on her shoulders. You should be laughing, frolicking, discoing the evenings away, sharing the night with—"

"You?" Blythe interjected dryly. "Is this one of many well-rehearsed lines, Mr. Smith?"

Cad straightened up and sat cross-legged. "Can that Mr. Smith stuff, will you, Sky Eyes? We know each other a bit too well for that."

"One kiss doesn't constitute an affair."

"But many affairs begin with an incendiary kiss." His gaze was leveled steadily at her when he added, "And I'm not handing you a line. You're too smart for that, and you can't deny that we connected. Not if you're honest with yourself."

Blythe sighed. "You're making too much out of a kiss. It was just the result of proximity and propinquity—"

"My foot. Are you going to tell me you'd have kissed any man who walked into your room? I don't believe it. Give up, Sky Eyes. It was instant combustion for both of us."

Unwilling to deny the truth, Blythe chose to ignore his words. "Will you stop calling me Sky Eyes?"

"Why? It's the truth. You have the bluest eyes and the reddest hair and the most luscious peaches-and-cream complex—"

"Stop!" Blythe catapulted from her seat. Lucas had always complimented her on her complexion, which he'd likened to a fresh peach. He'd often told her she'd never grow old, just as she'd never tan. She would just mature and turn as lovely as a peach in full fruition.

"Ah. I hit a nerve," Cad said, also standing. "Did the old boyfriend tell you how beautiful you are? Did you have a fight with him?"

"Not boyfriend. Husband."

Cad's expression went rigid. His back became ramrod straight, and Blythe suddenly could see the steel she'd sensed deep within him.

"I didn't know you were married."

About ready to walk out, Blythe hesitated. She despised her vacillation, but had to acknowledge a genuine curiosity about the man standing so stiffly in front of her, composed of so many layers though he showed her only the outer, most superficial one. She wanted to dig deeper, just as he was doing with her.

"Would it have made any difference?"

His smile returned, but this time it didn't reach the golden-green eyes. His gaze remained watchful, unreadable. "Your prejudices are showing, Sky Eyes. You assume all ski bums have no money, no steady job, no respectability. No scruples."

Blythe shrugged. She didn't feel the criticism applied to her. She had escaped from that world in which appearances and superficial conviviality and status were everything, where society was organized into a subtle and elaborate caste system. The pariahs were not so visibly rejected as in India, but the polite exclusion was there. The unspoken repudiation.

"Your career—or lack of it—is your choice. I'm merely referring to your earlier statements, about champagne greetings and combining athletic with sexual exercise," she told him finally.

He moved closer to her, until she could breathe in his potent male odor combined with woodsy after shave that elusively teased her nostrils. She stood her ground and resisted the impact of his virility.

"Don't you know when I'm teasing?" he demanded. "Do you really think I would equate you with the meaningless affairs I've had in my checkered past?"

Her chin went up. "If those affairs were meaningless, that doesn't say much for you. I don't like men who indulge indiscriminately. It signals a lack of maturity and restraint."

"So beneath that cool exterior exists a hardened moral arbiter? Men don't have the corner on expeditious, casual relationships. And it takes a while for a man to sow his wild oats. Some never do. And they never grow up. But if you follow your instincts, Sky Eyes, you'll see that both of us could have a no-holds-barred, earth-shaking affair."

"And that's exactly what I don't want," Blythe said sharply, biting her full lower lip immediately. Why had she revealed that? He was bound to pounce on it.

He did.

Taking her hands in his, he led her gently back to the chair. But he didn't push her down. "Why don't you tell me about it, Blythe?" he coaxed gently. "Tell me what's locked up inside you."

This time there was no coercion. He waited for her decision, and although she knew she was not being entirely logical, entirely reasonable, she considered telling him the truth. She was following her instincts, and they were telling her that he really wanted to know. That he was genuinely interested. She could see the concern in his eyes.

For a minute, her resolution faltered, and she debated keeping him in suspense as to whether she was married. She could always go back up that beautiful staircase and let him stew over it all night. His performance at the party merited that kind of treatment.

But another look into his eyes pierced the icy shell that had surrounded her. Perhaps she ought to break her self-imposed silence. The old belief that it was easier to confide in strangers seemed to hold true now. Except that deep inside she did not feel that Cad was a stranger.

She sat down and leaned back in the chair, her hands in Cad's strong, broad ones.

"I'm a widow."

His hands tightened on hers, and she could feel relief work through his entire body. His golden-green eyes darkened. "You had me going there for a minute."

She put her head back and closed her eyes, trying to gather her thoughts. Hesitantly, she began to tell Cad about Lucas, about his senseless death.

"The following day was his birthday, and I was throwing him a party. I suddenly realized we didn't have enough beverages, so I asked Lucas to get some juice and soda. The store was only a few blocks away, and since Lucas hated sports, he used to walk as often as he could to stay fit. A little boy broke away from his mother just as Lucas was about to cross the street. The mother was carrying the child's baby brother in her arms, and nobody else was close enough to help. Lucas ran into the street and pushed the little boy to safety, but he was run over by a car that couldn't stop in time." Her voice lowered as she fought to keep it even. "Lucas died in the hospital before I could reach his side."

Cad's hands exerted a sympathetic pressure, and she lifted her head, looking at him. "How long ago did your husband pass away?"

"Eleven months, three weeks, and five days. The day after tomorrow is his birthday."

Cad nodded. "And you thought you'd get away, come to terms with his death."

She smiled wanly. "That was the general idea. I wanted to put behind me all the confused, jumbled feelings that I still experience, even after all these months."

"Are you still bitter?"

"I guess a part of me will always be. At first, I was very bitter. I was angry at the young mother for letting her son get away, at the child who ran into the street, at the hospital for not being able to pull Lucas through, at the police for not notifying me earlier so I could at least have been at his side when he died. At the whole world, eventually, for the injustice. And most of all, at myself, for having asked Lucas to go out while I took care of some other preparations."

Cad got up and sat on the wide arm of the chair, putting his arm about her shoulders. "But surely you can see that no one was really at fault—especially not you. It was a tragic accident."

"Rationally, I suppose I knew that. But emotionally, I wanted to blame somebody. I was finally able to come to terms with my grief, get over the anger, and stop lashing out at myself and others. Work was my panacea, and after a few weeks I was able to sleep nights, at least for a few hours at a time." Pausing, a lump of lingering pain blocking her speech, she didn't tell Cad that until very recently the old nightmare had still been making its regular appearance. Basking in his warmth and security, she looked up at him, trying out a watery smile. "I'm all right," she told him bravely.

Cad squeezed her shoulder, and said softly, "Lucas must have been quite a man."

Her eyes took on a hazy, reminiscing quality, and she answered quietly, "He was. Worth every bit of sacrifice we had to make that first year."

At Cad's raised eyebrows, she elaborated. "When I decided to marry Lucas, my family was vehemently opposed. Not only was he poor, but his training in social work was socially unacceptable. The way my parents saw it, if I had to marry a working man, I could at least have picked a doctor or lawyer." She stared thoughtfully into the leaping flames, finding their fiery energy soothing. "But somebody going for his Ph.D. part time—and horror of horrors, driving a taxi to pay for his education—why, that was unthinkable to the Bedfords."

Cad listened silently, attentively, absorbing her every word as the fire seemed to absorb the echo of her voice in the quiet, deserted room. "Lucas was from the Midwest. When he asked me to follow him there, I did, even though I knew that meant severing my ties with my family. My parents warned me they'd never send us a penny. But I was obdurate. I loved Lucas, and couldn't care less about money. As far as I was concerned, the less money we had, the happier we'd be."

"Are you sure you didn't marry Lucas to get away from your family, as an act of rebellion?"

Blythe sat up, removing his arm from her shoulders. "No, I did not," she told him in a low, furious tone. "Lucas had a B.A. in philosophy, but he didn't just philosophize about the world and its problems. He actually set out to do something about it. And I admired as well as loved him."

Cad's expression was still skeptical, and she asked abruptly, "Why do you hate rich people?"

He considered her question for a moment. "It's not rich people *per se* I hate. Or even wealth. Money can buy comfort and security, if not happiness. But my experiences with one particular kind of rich person— of rich woman—has not been very positive. She was grasping, and she looked on social climbing and amassing wealth as a career in itself, to the exclusion of everything else in life. Nothing stood in her way, and if she thought treachery was necessary, she'd stoop to that. Even to the point of bartering her body."

"That's a very harsh statement," Blythe said after a moment. "Don't you think you might have misjudged the person who's made you feel this way?"

"One person clinched it, but I've seen others like her."

His bitterness surprised her. "I still think you might have been too harsh on her. It's not only women who get seduced by money and power. I hated the whole scene, the hypocrisy and keeping up of appearances, the fake emotions and overwhelming materialism." Feeling a lot better after her painful disclosure, discovering that it did help to share the pain, she added, "Not all rich people are like that, of course, but that was my experience in my own charmed circle." Essaying a smile, she added, "That's why a ski bum with no pretensions is such a breath of fresh air, even though he scandalizes poor unsuspecting women and has unfortunate caveman tendencies."

Cad smiled, but she felt something in him had changed. His gaze seemed guarded, and she could sense that he felt uneasy.

The degree of awareness between them shocked her. She had come to Indian Cove to put the past behind her, but she was not yet ready to start building a future. Too many conflicting emotions still beset her. And it would take time to put her emotional house in order.

Rising, she told Cad, "I'm going upstairs. I'm a bit tired."

Cad straightened. "I'll walk you to your room."

She smiled. "No, thanks. I don't think I'll get lost or mugged on the way there. Everyone seems to be sleeping soundly after that feast." Impulsively, she stood on tiptoe to drop a quick kiss on his cheek.

"Thanks for listening."

Before he could respond, she left the room, turning on the staircase to glance quickly back.

Cad's back was stiff, his muscles rigid beneath the green sweater, his legs braced far apart, his outline bathed in the light from the fire.

His expression of deep thoughtfulness stayed with her as she undressed for the second time that night. Indeed, it stayed with her even when she had donned her nightgown and lay under the covers, eyes closed. Fleetingly, she thought it was just as well. She would be seeing no more of Cad Smith after the next few days.

CHAPTER SIX

BLYTHE SAW THE man approaching swiftly on foot, striding purposefully through the snow, his black-clad body a dark outline against the sea of white. This time she was not surprised that Cad had hunted her down. There had been an unfinished quality about their talk last night—actually, a few hours ago—and she knew that was due mostly to her abrupt departure.

But she hadn't been able to help it. After Lucas, she had thought she could never have that kind of sensitivity toward a man again. And even with Lucas it had taken her a while to be able to anticipate his moods and thoughts. She'd just met Cad, and while she was not yet able to read his thoughts—he was more inscrutable than her husband, despite the care-free front he presented to the world—she was keenly aware of his moods.

As he closed the distance between them, Blythe wondered if he was going to confide to her what had been bothering him toward the end of their talk. She found him a man of contradictions, of mystery even. But she was sure of two things: He kept his word, and he had little in common with the people she'd left behind when she married Lucas.

As he reached her side, all was still around them.

"I thought I'd find you here." He looked about them, at the dark, mysterious forest that encroached on three sides and at the half-frozen waterfall. "Most people stay on the marked trails. Not too many like to explore this far."

Blythe looked at him curiously. "You know every inch of this land, don't you?"

He smiled. "Indian Cove is my home away from home. I've been to ski resorts all over the world, and this is one of my two favorites. The other one is in Europe."

By mutual, silent accord, they approached the creek, where soft gurgles could be heard beneath the ice. Blythe inhaled deeply of the clean, biting air, giddy with the fairy-tale beauty of their surroundings . . . and with Cad's nearness.

"I've given some thought to what you said last night, Blythe." She looked at him and found him staring straight ahead, unseeing, his gaze turned inward. Today he was dressed all in black, and he looked like a Norse god in mourning. "I've seen the sickness myself—terminal materialism, the insatiable hunger for power, the blind accumulation of wealth. Only in my case, it took very real, personal form—the woman

I was engaged to. Oh, she did her best to hide her true nature, assuming the guise of Lady Bountiful and doing charity work."

Blythe stared at him. "Are you sure there wasn't more to her than what you acknowledge? Maybe she really was dedicated to her charity work. She could have become deeply involved with the people she was helping."

Cad laughed shortly, a rough, bitter sound. "Alessandra dedicated? To herself, yes. To anyone else, no. She was supposed to marry me, but she preferred working on her pet project to being with me."

"And do you think every woman should give up what she loves, what she's worked toward, just to be with her man? There is no conflict, Cad, if a woman is content staying at home. But there have been too many changes in our culture to expect that of *all* women nowadays. Some companies are beginning to deal with that. Instead of just arbitrarily transferring their managers, they're looking for alternate solutions."

"I'm afraid I'm the old-fashioned type, then," Cad said, but a golden gleam was twinkling in his eyes. Blythe guessed that he had begun to put the painful memory behind him.

"I see. Your wife—and children, should you have them—would have to follow you on the ski trail? Makes a lot of sense to me."

Cad opened his mouth to say something, then closed it. "It might have made a difference if Alessandra had been truly dedicated to her charity work. But Alessandra always looked out for Alessandra." He put his booted foot on one of the boulders that dotted the riverbank, and leaned his elbow on his knee. "What would your husband have thought if you'd become involved in some charity work? What would your parents have said?"

"My parents!" Her eyes clouded. The curtain of memories shrouded her once again. They had been violently opposed to her work at the institute, just as they'd been opposed to her marriage. They'd attempted a reconciliation after Lucas died, thinking they could bring her back into the fold, hoping that she would continue the Bedford traditions, since her brother Harlan showed no signs of settling down, and she doubted he ever would. She had flatly rejected their attempts to reclaim her, and they'd warned her she'd have to come to her senses soon.

Something wet and heavy hit her in the middle of her chest, spraying white, crystalline powder into her neck and face. Startled, she automatically brushed it from her chin and nose, and looked blindly at Cad.

He was grinning at her, his expression wickedly dangerous, and she saw a huge snowball in his hands. He was already preparing to throw it, going through the movements in exaggerated slow motion.

Her gloomy thoughts undraped themselves from her, just as he'd no doubt intended, and Blythe felt laughter gurgle in her throat. It felt foreign there, since she'd had little reason to laugh since Lucas's death.

For an instant, she stood motionless. God, she missed him. And part of her always would. She felt guilty for enjoying herself.

But another snowball departed Cad's hand with the speed of a bullet. The force of it sent her backwards,

and she found herself sitting in the snow. She got up
to retaliate, thinking that the time for grief was over.
Lucas would want her to be happy. He would be the
last person to demand that she keep a grieving vigil
over him.

Her gloved hands closed over a clump of the fine,
cold powder. Quickly rolling it into a tennis-ball-sized
missile, she got to her feet and advanced. Cad bent
down to pick up more snow, and when he straightened, she pitched.

Unfortunately, he was also prepared, and a soft
white ball hit her lightly in the face. She choked,
rubbing her hand over her mouth, which was full of
snow.

"You all right?" Cad asked.

"Just fine," Blythe answered, already planning her
revenge strategy.

During the next few minutes, a fierce war ensued
in which there was neither victor nor vanquished. At
the end of it, both Blythe and Cad plopped down onto
the snow to catch their breath. They were covered
from head to toe in white, their caps long gone in the
snowball struggle.

Blythe lay in the snow for a long moment, looking
up at the bright blue patches of sky visible among the
canopy of pine trees sheltering them.

She sighed, feeling the magic of the spot seep into
her very pores. She turned her head and saw Cad
propped up on one elbow, his gaze changed from the
gentle teasing of the past half-hour to the suddenly
intense smoldering of desire. Slowly, reluctantly, she
rose for the walk back to the lodge.

* * *

"Shh," Cad said, putting his arm about her shoulders as they neared another tiny stream nearly a mile from the waterfall. He suddenly tensed at her side and pointed. "There she is."

Blythe looked, and felt her heart turn over. Memories of Bambi crowded in her brain as she saw the doe and fawn approach the stream, their eyes alert, their movements delicate. The brown heads bent low, the elegant lines of their bodies prepared for flight, and Blythe held her breath.

She and Cad remained silent, motionless, as the deer daintily drank from the partly frozen stream. Their nervous, skittery departure released their human observers from immobility.

Blythe turned to Cad, her eyes shining. "Thanks, Cad. That was beautiful."

His eyes lingered on her face, his gaze like a caress. Suddenly, he smiled and pulled at her hand.

"Let's go. I'll race you back."

It was an interesting sort of race. They chased each other through the snow and Cad ran circles around her, teasing her, challenging her.

At one point, she stopped to catch her breath, laughing joyfully, and Cad closed the gap between them, leaning toward her. He took off her orange cap and buried one hand in the tumbling mass of her hair, pressing on the back of her head to pull her closer to him.

Their eyes met the instant before their lips did. His kiss was soft, tender, with no raw passion this time. It was a shared moment of tenderness, of wordless communion.

He replaced her cap and brushed wisps of hair from her cheeks, his fingers feather light on her face. He traced the line of her delicate nose, then ran a fingertip over the lines of her full mouth. Blythe felt as if the last layer of the ice that had so long encrusted her feelings was slowly melting and disappearing forever.

Then he drew back and started to run, plowing effortlessly through one mound of snow, leaping over another, calling over his shoulders for her to get moving.

She secured the cap on her head and followed him at a sprint.

The next two days were idyllic. Blythe called Justin, telling him of her decision to stay, and he was pleased. He told her not to worry, that he and Gladys would hold down the fort.

She did see Stan Martin the following day, but since Cad was with her, the conversation was of necessity short. Stan told her where he lived and worked, his eyes casting a challenge at Cad's stony face, and told her to look him up if she should find herself in Iowa.

"You know, Cad, you should try to be a bit more civil," Blythe told him as she watched Stan's stiff back departing from the dining room.

"Why? He's competition, and I don't like competition. There's no need to pretend politeness when I know he's trying to cut in on my territory."

Blythe leaned back, amused. Sipping some coffee after the delicious lunch of shrimp cocktail, steak, and

Russian salad, she asked, "Are we reverting to the primitive territorial imperative here? I thought that had died with the emergence of *Homo erectus*."

His grin slashed a line of white on his bronzed face. "I doubt it will ever entirely leave the male of the species. After all, we *are* animals."

"Civilized animals, let's hope," she told him as she got up. "And just remember that I *do* have a choice. I'm flattered by your interest, as long as it stops short of a need to own me. I have a mind, and I use it. I can make decisions for myself."

She left Cad sitting bemused at the table. She knew he was not used to that kind of treatment. She didn't believe he'd exaggerated too much when he'd said women flocked to him. Even if his self-assurance, golden good looks, and piratical air were not enough, there was the added attraction of his romantic lifestyle.

That evening, after they ate an excellent dinner and sipped some brandy by the fire in the company of fellow lodgers, Cad suggested a walk. Blythe was intrigued, and went upstairs to change from her blouse and woolen skirt into warm pants, a sweater, and her parka.

As their boots crunched in the snow, moonlight spilling all about them, Blythe had to acknowledge Cad's imagination and strategic restraint. He hadn't pushed her, but she didn't think his patience was only a subtle maneuver on his part. He might possess expertise and experience, but she suspected that beneath the charming, powerful exterior lay a vein of sensitivity. He knew instinctively that power tactics would not work with her, so he was courting her slowly and delicately. But she also knew that he respected her grief. As a matter of fact, she believed that Cad was a nicer fellow than anyone not very close to him could suspect.

"You know, this is certainly original," she remarked. "A midnight moonlit snow trek instead of a midnight swim."

He stopped her at the edge of the forest. They were far from the resort now, and seemed to exist in a world of their own in the quiet winter wonderland.

"One does what one can with what's available."

His teasing response did not fool her. "I see. So this is an old ploy, a calculated effort to get me into bed with you?"

Her back was against a tree trunk, and he leaned forward, his hands trapping her against the rough bark.

"I'd like to get you into bed. I think you'll look beautiful between my sheets—all vibrant color against the white." Her breath caught in her throat at his vivid image, and his hands descended to caress her neck. "But when we make love, it won't be out of cold calculation. It will be out of hot passion. And mutual consent. You're too much a woman to have it otherwise, and I think too much of you to want it any other way."

She felt a snowflake on her nose and tilted her face to receive its companions. Laughter gurgled in her throat like a crystalline brook, penetrating the silence of night with tinkling purity.

"Thank you, Cad. Thank you for these marvelous days. Even if we did meet in an unorthodox manner, and even though your conduct has not been impeccable."

"That's why you like me. Because you're tired of

stuffed shirts and want to be with a real man."

"I think Stan Martin's a real man, too," she teased him deliberately.

His fingers slid inside the collar of her turtleneck, their coldness turning to instant heat against her skin, starting a trail of fire that worked its incendiary path downward to her toes.

"I agree," he growled. "But I saw you first."

"There you go again. I don't get a say in the matter."

"Destiny has already had its say." He spoke against her lips before covering her mouth with his.

As his lips played with hers, roaming from corner to corner, nipping the sensitive skin between upper lip and nose, descending to nibble on her chin before taking her full lower lip into his mouth, she was warmly inclined to agree with him.

But she pushed at his shoulders, trying to fight the nebulous mists of desire that were clouding her brain and impeding her capacity to reason.

"Cad, please, stop," she told him, moving her head to one side as she evaded his hungry mouth.

His grip tightened slightly on her neck, his thumbs pressing into soft crevices behind her ears. And then he was leaning his forehead against hers.

She let her arms slide from his chest, where they'd been frantically pushing as she'd tried to stem his passion and her own. "When . . . when are you going back to work?" she asked.

She could feel his smile against her skin. "I *am* at work."

She smiled, too. "I'm talking about your other passion—skiing. Will you be participating in any events, or will you take a temporary job?"

He lifted his head to gaze down at her in the ivory spill of moonlight. "I told you, I *am* at work. I own this resort."

Her clear, flutelike laugh sliced through the night air again. "Come on, Cad. You don't have to invent a secure, nine-to-five job for me. You know I'm not impressed with money or position or status. One of the things I like about you is the fact that you're not money-hungry. And I'm not attracted to you because you're a glamorous ski bum, but because of all the other things I've found out about you, the things you don't flaunt—your sense of humor, your gentleness and understanding. Your spontaneity is worth more to me than a large bank account and innumerable assets."

Cad went suddenly still, his hands dropping to her waist. He was about to tell her something, Blythe knew. Something important. She could tell from the sudden seriousness of his expression.

But then the moment passed, and she realized that he had changed his mind. He was not going to reveal anything. A large, impudent snowflake broke into the tenseness of her own waiting piercing through the suspense, and Cad growled, "Woman, I have to have you. Too many moons of abstinence have passed."

He wrestled her to the ground and they rolled around in the fresh-fallen snow, surrounded by a world of white that veiled them from head to toe and curtained them with silent, mystical intimacy.

He finally pinned her to the ground, his body covering hers, his head hovering above her face for an intense, erotically charged instant.

Then his lips swooped down. This time his tongue

penetrated her welcoming parted lips, finding her own tongue and mating with it, and finally biting on it gently.

Blythe moaned, and her hands went around Cad's neck. She could feel him bow-taut above her, his body rigid with restraint. The kiss continued for a blissful eternity, and then Cad rolled off her, sliding onto his back to breathe in large gulps of air. His fingers dug into the snow and gathered a handful, which he rubbed into his face.

"This will have to do till I get to an icy shower," he told her, rolling toward her again and burying his face in the sweetness of her throat. He tasted her skin and left a spine-tingling sensation there before rising in one smooth motion and extending a hand. "Sky Eyes, I promised you I would never hurt you or scare you again, but you've got to cooperate. If you continue to lie there in the snow like a delicious meal, this starving man is going to eat you."

Blythe stretched, and after a deliberate delay, accepted his hand. His pull almost catapulted her to her feet.

"Where's that famed self-restraint?" she asked as she began to brush the snow from her slacks and jacket. "And by all accounts—including yours—you can't be starving. It can't have been *that* long between meals."

His gaze glittered, delivering a sensual message that bore deep into her innermost parts. That message was reinforced by the verbal assault his husky words launched on her brain.

"Sky Eyes, there's hunger, and there's starvation.

And I couldn't satisfy my appetite for you at one sitting. Or one meal. You would take continual devouring."

CHAPTER SEVEN

"Want to go for another run?"

Blythe leaned over, hands on her knees, back bent, to relieve the cramping of muscles long underused.

"No," she gasped. "I think I've had enough for today."

Cad knelt at her foot to release the catches and divest her of her skis.

"Kind of soft, aren't you?" he said as he straightened.

"Only in some things," she shot back.

He gazed at her, and she stared back. She was grateful to Cad. Yesterday had been the anniversary of Lucas's death, and Cad had helped her forget by planning a day so full of activities that her head had spun. But the distractions had prevented her from thinking—at least during the day. At night she'd still been torn by memories, but had found it easier to let go. She had finally come to terms with her husband's death. And with her own life, which she planned to lead with her old enthusiasm and joy.

But there was danger in the immediate, strong attraction between herself and Cad. Blythe was fully aware that her feelings for him might be merely an infatuation, and she needed time to put things into perspective before either of them got hurt.

"Are you sure you can't stay another week?"

Her desire to stay with him was so intense that Blythe knew she had to let things cool. She had to let her feelings climb off the roller coaster Cad had sent them hurtling over.

"I'm sure, Cad. This has been a wonderful idyll, but I have work to do. I've stayed too long as it is."

His eyes told her it had not been long enough for him. Her body agreed. But her mind had to make the decision. And it had to be a rational, sensible one.

"Meet me in the lobby for lunch, okay?" he said. "Say in an hour? That should give us time to shower and change. I want to take a shot at Suicide Run before I go upstairs."

She nodded. "Be careful, okay?" she told him, knowing she wouldn't see him for a while . . . if ever again. This was the best way.

He cupped her cheek. "Hey, you're talking to an expert here, remember? A world-class skier. See you in an hour."

Impulsively, she grabbed his head and brought it down for a fierce kiss.

"See you." Then she turned and headed for the room clerk's desk, trying to walk as quickly as possible although weighted down with her skis and poles. She didn't want Cad to see the suspicious wetness in her eyes.

"Blythe!"

About to climb into the taxi, Blythe halted. She had wanted to leave without this confrontation. But she couldn't ignore Cad's voice. She just couldn't turn her back on him and calmly drive off.

She turned toward him, and he ran the rest of the way to her.

"You were going to leave without saying goodbye?" His eyes scanned the suitcase the cab driver was stowing in the trunk, and the overnight bag she held in her hand. His voice was incredulous, and laced with its hoarse throatiness was hurt.

"I left you a note."

"How nice," he said sarcastically. "And what does the note say?"

Blythe looked toward the cab. The driver was back inside, and the meter was running.

Cad shoved his hand in his pocket and took out his wallet. Giving the driver a twenty-dollar bill, he said, "Here." Turning to Blythe, he told her, "Now you don't have to worry about the fare while you tell me why you're hightailing it out of here."

Anger had replaced the hurt in his tone. She couldn't blame him, but he had to see that parting wasn't easy for her, either. She told him so.

"Really? And if it's so goddamn hard for you to

leave, why are you going? Or were you just taken in by the ski-bum glamour, too?"

Her head shot up. "You know better than that. But you have to see that I've just become reconciled to my loss. I'm not ready for another relationship, Cad. I came to Indian Cove for rest and relaxation, and meditation. Things have been going too fast. For both of us."

"Not for me," he denied, his hand gripping her arm and bringing her body close to his.

She reacted instantly. The chemistry was there, potent and magical.

She sighed; but her sigh sounded more like a soft groan. "I'm not denying we're attracted to each other, Cad. But you have to see that it's no good. Everything was too sudden, came too close on the heels of my acceptance of Lucas's death and my decision to start really living again. I want to be fair to both of us. I have to find out my true feelings for you."

"And how do you propose to do that?" His voice was flat, his eyes unfathomable.

"By going away. In the note I wrote to you, I told you that if you still feel the same way, we can meet here three months from now."

"Won't your work keep you away?"

"If we both want to come, nothing will keep either of us away." She essayed a smile. "it will be fitting. In three months there'll be the beginning of spring thaws, signaling the rebirth of—"

"I don't need anything to symbolize my feelings for you. I know what I feel for you now, Blythe. And my feelings won't be any different in three months."

"Then you can wait, can't you?" she said softly. "And you can help me out by giving me time to sort through my feelings?"

He didn't answer. "Give me your address."

She shook her head. "It'll be better if I don't, Cad. I'll see you here in three months."

He stared at her a moment longer, then released her arm. Turning, he headed back to the lodge.

"Cad!"

She didn't want to end like this. She didn't want him to think that she'd used him. She started to run after him. Then the thought occurred to her that perhaps he'd only been idly flirting with her. But it went against everything she believed about him, against her deepest instinct.

Then, why had he turned away? She'd tried to explain. He'd been understanding until now.

Perhaps his feelings did not run that deep. Perhaps it had been his male ego talking. Maybe he felt resentful because he hadn't taken her to bed. Perhaps he'd just been angry because she was leaving so abruptly. Was that why he'd asked her to stay? When she refused, had he simply lost interest?

She couldn't bring herself to believe any of her conjectures. But the fact she was even thinking them proved that she and Cad did not know each other very well. After several years of marriage to Lucas she'd been able to predict most of his actions. Their marital ESP had been quite fully developed.

Swallowing her disappointment, pushing away her thoughts of Cad and the empty feeling that assailed her, she got into the taxi and forced herself to think of the grant, of the children, of stingy, incompetent Vincent Nimms, who held so much power in his hands.

The hilly Wisconsin land passed in a brilliant white blur while she was lost in her thoughts.

"Good morning, Gladys," Blythe said as she entered her office at the institute the following day.

Gladys quickly put down the floppy disc she was about to feed to her word processor and came over to hug her. "Hi, Blythe. Good to have you back. How come you came in so early?"

Blythe looked at Gladys with affection. Her secretary was deceptively feminine—petite, blond, with huge hazel eyes and a slender, almost fragile figure. But underneath the apparent fragility and the soft dresses and skirts Gladys liked to wear lay a will of steel and an astonishing capacity for work.

She also had the kind of loyalty that kept her at a job that utilized her many skills but did not pay her what she could have earned at a larger corporation. Glady's last raise had been minimal. Blythe had wished it could be more, but finances were very tight and she could not afford to increase Gladys's salary to a level commensurate with her ability, hard work, and dedication.

"I might ask you the same question," Blythe said, putting her briefcase down on a spotless edge of Gladys's desk while she went to the coffeemaker in the corner and poured herself a cup of coffee. "Milk or black today?" she asked, knowing that Gladys's preferences changed daily.

"Black, please." That meant she'd taken the time

to eat breakfast today. "So how did it go at Indian Cove?"

The innocent question sent a shaft of pain through Blythe. She had not realized how much she would miss Cad. Had not wanted to think that she could ever miss him so badly.

She was spared the trouble of answering when Justin Harris appeared around the corner.

"Well, the prodigal returns," he exclaimed cheerfully, coming over to drop a kiss on her cheek and pour himself a cup of coffee.

"Have you two been coming in early every day since I left?" Blythe demanded. "And working much too hard, as usual?"

"Well, someone has to work around here. You left us all by ourselves, while you relaxed and frolicked in the . . . snow."

Without meaning to, Justin had hit the bull's-eye. Although she tried to fight it, Blythe could feel a betraying warmth climb into her cheeks, and Justin's brown eyes were too sharp to miss the change.

"Ho, ho, so she *did* do some frolicking," he told Gladys, giving her an exaggerated wink. "Of what type, Blythe? And with whom? Tell all to Uncle Justin."

She unwrapped the arm that had encircled her shoulders as Justin exhorted her to make a full confession. Gladys, her eyes full of mischief, joined his efforts.

"Stop it, you two," Blythe said, attempting a severe tone and failing miserably. She'd never been a stern management type. "We can discuss my *skiing* and *hiking"*—she emphasized the two words, ignoring the good-natured ribbing she was receiving—"after I take care of all my mail and come up with an alternative proposal for Vincent Nimms."

The mere mention of his name threw a damper on the teasing. They all sobered up, and Gladys went around the desk to take out her operating system disc and insert a blank one for the day's work.

"By the way, Blythe," Gladys said, picking up a stack of pink telephone slips, "somewhere among these messages are a few phone calls from your parents. Penelope was quite disgruntled when I told her you were out of town."

"My mother expects everyone to be right by the phone when she calls," Blythe said dryly, walking over to Gladys's desk and retrieving the slips. "Anything urgent?"

Gladys handed her a smaller stack of messages, as Justin said, "I need to talk to you today. When can we meet?"

Blythe looked up from the messages she was riffling through and answered, "Can it wait till later in the day? I have to get back to some of these callers this morning."

Justin nodded and went to his office, and Blythe noticed Gladys's eyes following him wistfully until he disappeared around the corner.

Blythe looked down at the slips before Gladys could notice what she'd observed, and told herself she should have seen this happening. Gladys was a logical, sensible woman, not given to flights of fancy. Blythe knew the love shining in those hazel eyes had not blossomed overnight, or during the short time she'd been away. It had to have been growing for a while, and she just hadn't noticed. She'd been too immersed in the problems of running the institute on less than adequate funds, and in her own grief. She wondered if Justin returned Gladys's affection.

She looked up from her telephone messages to find Gladys regarding her quizzically. "The mail is in your bin," she said.

"Thank you, Gladys. I guess I'm just postponing the moment when I'll have to talk to my parents," she improvised. It was not entirely false, either.

The phone rang.

"Institute for Disabled Children, Ms. Jameson speaking." Gladys's round, pretty face twisted into a grimace as she looked up at Blythe. "Your mother," she mouthed.

Blythe nodded toward her office. As she walked into it, she could hear Gladys using the placating voice that salesmen use on customers when they've sold them a lemon or made exaggerated claims about a product. Blythe squared her shoulders like a soldier going into combat. Verbal combat, in this instance.

As she drove home that evening, Blythe thought back on her angry, heated words with Penelope Bedford. She had invited her parents to tour the institute, to see how much its work was needed, to have them witness the joy, promise, and courage of these children. But Penelope reminded Blythe that her father, who'd had a mild case of polio as a child, and still carried emotional scars from the trauma, couldn't bear

the sight of infirmity. Surely, Blythe had some consideration for her father's feelings? Penelope demanded, going on to reiterate an additional reason
why she and her husband would not come out to the
Midwest.

Even Blythe's account of young Timmy Singer,
who had become disabled in the car accident that had
claimed his parents' and his older sister's lives, could
not cut through Penelope's inflexible opposition. Finally, furious, Blythe had exploded. She'd told her
mother and father—who was on the extension—that
sickness knew no social boundaries and that accidents
did not distinguish between fat and thin bank accounts.
She was committed to these children, and she was not
going to abandon them.

Her mother, as always, had closed with a decla-
ration that Blythe would eventually come to her senses
and take her rightful position as a Bedford heiress.
At least she'd kept the Bedford name after she married
"that man."

Blythe had not bothered to remind her mother one
more weary time that her decision to keep the Bedford
name had nothing to do with loyalty to the Bedford
family, that she had made that choice only because
neither she nor Lucas had believed that marriage was
a reason to abandon one's name. He didn't want to
become Mr. Bedford, and didn't feel he should ask
her to abandon her identity and become Mrs. Wain-
wright. They were both individuals, and their marriage had been founded on something other than
Blythe's surrendering her maiden name. It had meant
more than the marriage license they had been issued—

the commitment had lain in both of them.

As she parked her car and entered her small, comfortable apartment—the institute was located in La Crosse, Wisconsin, not far from the Iowa–Minnesota state line—she forced the unpleasant thoughts out of her weary mind. She was glad to be home. After Lucas's death she had moved into a smaller apartment, partly to erase the memories that had attacked her with painful regularity, but mostly to economize—and it had become a sanctuary from outside problems.

She wasn't very hungry, but she fixed herself some tomato soup and a salad with bits of cheese and ham thrown in as an afterthought—and sat down in her old, decrepit rocking chair to think over the day's events and the letter Gladys had given her that afternoon.

Gladys worked for both Blythe and Justin, and Blythe knew it must have been hard for the secretary to bring herself to show Blythe the letter. But Blythe had thanked Gladys warmly, telling her she'd done the right thing.

The letter made clear that Justin had been offered a very lucrative position as head of an organization that handled funds for various social services. The job would certainly utilize his considerable skills to better capacity than his position at the institute, and the salary was more than twice what Blythe was paying him. Yet she was convinced that Justin would turn the job offer down.

Which meant she had to tell him that she could dispense with his services. Justin shouldn't let his great loyalty block his career advancement any further. He'd done a lot for the institute—but it was time he did something for himself as well as for others.

She decided to have dinner with him later in the week, ostensibly to discuss business and the result of her meeting with Vincent Nimms. Then she would ask him about the offer.

The next few days were hectic, and Blythe and Gladys barely had time to breathe, coming in early and staying late. To top it off, one of the nurses quit and the physical therapist came down with the flu.

And her meeting with Vincent Nimms was canceled.

As she fought her way through the blizzard that had suddenly descended on them late in the afternoon, Blythe found a few choice epithets for Nimms. It wasn't hard. The man inspired all sorts of colorful language.

She decided not to go home to shower and change. The storm had, of course, waited to make its sudden appearance until right before the rush hour, ensuring that work crews could not clear the roads in time to prevent a traffic jam. At a snail's pace, she drove to the restaurant where she was to join Justin for their dinner meeting.

She would rather have postponed the get-together, but Justin had left early that day to take care of some personal business downtown, and she didn't know where to reach him. He was probably making his own way to the restaurant, and she couldn't just not show up.

It took her an hour to reach the restaurant. As she'd anticipated, Justin was already there.

He waved her over to his table and smiled warmly. Within minutes, he had ordered, and a waiter had placed their salads and wedges of luscious-looking melon before them.

They discussed business first, then the rotten weather and its despicable timing, and finally, over the main dish, Blythe asked casually, "Are you going to accept that terrific job offer?"

Justin's fork stopped on its way to his mouth.

"What job offer?" he asked, feigning innocence.

"The one where you'll earn twice what I pay you. The job where your talents will be put to full use as director."

Justin bit into the piece of meat on his fork, but she was sure he was not tasting it. He chewed slowly, methodically, buying time. Finally, he asked, "How did you find out?"

Now Blythe hesitated, but she knew the truth would eventually come out. "Gladys."

He nodded. Worried that he might be upset with the secretary, Blythe said hurriedly, "Don't be mad at Gladys, Justin. She really means well and—"

He raised his eyes and looked at her with a hazy, faraway expression. "How could I be mad at her? I love her."

Blythe almost choked on her sip of wine and looked at him wonderingly. "Why, that's wonderful, Justin. I had no—"

He shrugged gloomily. "How can it be wonderful? She obviously wants me to leave. The sooner the better, it would appear."

Blythe opened her mouth to speak, remembering Gladys's loving expression, but she could not betray her friend's secret. The three of them were more than fellow workers; they had been drawn together by their fierce dedication to and love for the children, and they were very good friends. Besides, she could be mistaken about Gladys's feelings for Justin. Although she doubted it. Still, it was up to Gladys to disabuse Justin of his mistaken notion. It was up to the two of them to find out that they were in love with each other as well as with their work.

"You know, Justin," she said casually, after swallowing a delicious morsel of chicken, "I think you're wrong. I haven't seen any sign that Gladys wants you to go. Have you done anything to offend her?"

"Well, no, of course not. You know how Gladys is—so deceptively soft and feminine, but underneath she can be tough as nails when it comes to something she believes in. I'm sure she'd have chewed me out if I'd done something to anger her."

"There you have it," Blythe said, putting down her fork and sipping some wine. "If you haven't angered her or hurt her—and I agree with you that she'd have torn into you if you had—then she must have brought this job offer to my attention because she thinks it's too good an opportunity for you to pass up, which it is, of course." Her statement accomplished two purposes: it assured Justin that Gladys had not betrayed him, and it let him know that Blythe would not resent his decision to accept the job offer.

His next comment, however, dismayed her.

"Don't worry, Blythe. I'm not going to take it. I know how bogged down you are, how overworked and understaffed. You know me better than to think I'd desert you."

Blythe set her glass down. "But, Justin, you *must* leave," she told him earnestly. "I *want* you to take that job. It would be just perfect for you, with your interests and skills."

Justin took her hands in his. "Blythe, I'm not going anywhere until the institute is in the black. Certainly not until this grant business is resolved. I promised Lucas that if anything happened to him, I'd stay with you until I knew I wasn't needed, so I'm sticking."

Blythe felt her eyes fill with tears, and she blinked them away. "Justin, Lucas is dead, and nothing will ever bring him back. You've been more than a loyal friend; you've been almost a brother to me. Lucas would not expect you to stay any longer, not when this terrific opportunity has presented itself. He would have told you to go for it."

"Not if my leaving would hurt you. And if I leave now, you and the institute would be hurt. Lucas tried to be pragmatic, but at heart he was an idealist. And once you've known someone like Lucas and counted him as your friend, you can never go back to being grasping and self-indulgent." Smiling at his own words, he added, "I'm making myself sound like a martyr, and I didn't mean to. But I won't leave. And that's final."

One tear made it past Blythe's furious blinking, and Justin tenderly brushed it away. She glared at him, trying to be angry so she wouldn't indulge in this silly weeping.

"Justin Harris, you're inflating your own importance. I can take care of myself, for heaven's sake. I've been running the institute—"

"And running yourself ragged," Justin interrupted.

"I know you can take care of yourself, and you're doing a marvelous job, considering the difficulties you're encountering. But you're still understaffed, and the children would suffer if I left, particularly at this stage. I can't say the other job doesn't appeal to me— either in terms of salary or responsibilities—but I could never live with myself if I let you and the children down. The children need me a lot more than I need piles of money or a plush office. There'll be time for that later. And then I'll be able to live with my conscience."

Blythe squeezed his hands tightly, and she knew that was all he was going to say on the matter. She was immensely relieved, and at the same time deeply grateful to the quiet, unassuming man sitting across the table. Lucas had had a great capacity to endear himself to people. It had been a testament to his own integrity and loyalty to his friends that those who had known him continued to be loyal to him even after his death.

Since it was snowing heavily, Justin dropped her off at her apartment, promising to give her a lift to the institute in the morning and take her to the restaurant after work to pick up her car.

Justin asked subtle, and not so subtle, questions about Gladys on the slow, careful drive home. Blythe answered the questions in a way that would neither discourage Justin nor betray her other friend. It proved a tricky undertaking, and Blythe was glad when they stopped in front of her apartment.

Wanting to give him hope, she told Justin as she

opened the door on her side, "Don't give up hope. You two will make a lovely couple."

Justin laughed and dropped a kiss on her cheek, hugging her to him in a burst of exuberance. "I hope you're right, Blythe. I guess I should be encouraged that Gladys cared enough to interfere in my business. I'd never known her to open my personal mail before."

"That letter was addressed to you at the institute," Blythe managed weakly as he squeezed the air out of her lungs with his bear hug.

Justin let her go and said, "Addressed to *me*. Which reminds me that *you* didn't seem to have much trouble reading it, either."

Sensing dangerous waters, Blythe quickly slid out of the car. "See you tomorrow. Sweet dreams."

She could see that Justin's mock-menacing frown had quickly turned into a dreamy, faraway look. The same one she'd seen on Gladys's face the morning she returned from her vacation.

Mentally rubbing her hands at the happy fact that her instincts had been right and that romance was alive and well and blooming in Wisconsin, Blythe stopped herself short as she thought of her own romance.

But she shook her head, as if forcibly clearing thoughts of Cad away. There were still eleven weeks to go before their reunion, and she wanted to explore her new self. The frequency with which Cad turned up in her thoughts—particularly in the still of the night—was an indication of his importance to her. But she was determined to wait the whole eleven weeks.

As she stopped in front of her apartment door and

searched for her keys, she told herself she had no alternative in any case. She hadn't had the foresight to ask Cad for his address, and so would not know where to reach him. She could only hope that he'd still feel the same emotions for her in eleven weeks and would meet her in Indian Cove as the snow began to melt . . .

Opening the door, she let herself in and wearily put her purse down on the small table by the door.

Then alarm rippled through her, and her heart leaped to her throat as her hand flew back to pick up her purse and deal with the intruder sitting in the shadows in the living room.

"Hello, Sky Eyes," came a familiar voice in the darkness. "Nice wine, but I prefer red myself."

CHAPTER EIGHT

SHE FLIPPED A switch, and light flooded the room. Cad was sprawled in an armchair, his dark wool ski sweater with a geometric aquamarine pattern contrasting with the bright red and gold upholstery. In one hand, he held a glass half full of white wine. *Her* white wine. Since she hadn't opened a bottle lately, she knew he'd uncorked one of those she reserved for special occasions.

"What the hell are you doing here?" she asked, setting down her purse again and unconsciously straightening her white cape.

"Temper, temper," he answered, unfolding all six foot one of him from the chair that seemed to revive instantly as his weight was removed.

She pointed to the door. "Out!"

He assumed a plaintive expression, incongruous with his muscular build. But she was not about to let him bend her to his will and do with her as he wished.

"Out!" she repeated.

"Come on, Blythe. Have a heart. I have nowhere to go."

"I can give you several specific suggestions," she told him grimly. Then another thought occurred to her. "How did you get in here?"

He approached her to stand in front of her, and Blythe ignored the sudden fluctuations in her vital signs. She made herself pay close attention to his account.

"Mrs. Hooper."

"Mrs. Hooper?" she repeated, her eyes widening in disbelief. "But she's a very strict landlady who usually frowns on visitors of the opposite sex."

"I told her we were high school sweethearts," Cad said with a satisfied smile.

"And she bought it?" Esther Hooper was a small, suspicious woman in her early seventies, with a mind as sharp as a rapier.

"Well, I knew that if I tried to pass myself off as your brother or even as your cousin, I wouldn't stand a chance. She'd see straight through that." Even in the midst of her steadily mounting fury Blythe had to admire Cad's scheming mind and shrewd perception of people. "So I appealed to her romantic nature—"

"I didn't know she had one," Blythe muttered sourly.

"—and told her we'd been separated when I went to medical school and I'd been tracking you for fifteen years . . ."

"Fifteen years! Cad, I'm *only* twenty-seven."

"But I don't look to be in my mid-twenties," Cad explained reasonably, pausing in his incredible narrative to calmly sip some wine. "So I had to invent a span of time that would be believable to Mrs. Hooper. To further diminish the discrepancy in ages, I told her that you were a precocious child who had advanced three grades, and that you were a freshman when I was a senior." Finishing the wine, he added, "And I must say Esther Hooper's a charming lady. She was a veritable fountain of information."

Blythe pushed back her fur-lined white hood and tore off her woolen cape. "What kind of things did Mrs. Hooper reveal?" she asked, her eyes narrowed suspiciously.

Cad took the cape from her. "Oh, nothing too private or detailed, and nothing about your job. Just personal little things, about your habits and such, like how you like to ski and swim, and manage to kill almost every plant you come in contact with. Oh, and how you have a gentleman caller now and then who is just not right for you."

Blythe controlled the shiver of fury that traveled up her spine. "You know, Cad," she said in a forcibly controlled voice, "your name's definitely appropriate. Just who in hell gave you the right to invade my privacy?"

He smiled, shaking some of the rapidly melting snowflakes off her winter-white cape. "I'll have to turn up the thermostat now that you're here. I kept it real low until you returned," he remarked casually, heading for the bathroom. He stopped briefly to adjust the thermostat and said over his shoulder, "You know,

I didn't want to wait three months to see you. I want to get to know you better, and since you're not too forthcoming, my goal will be much more easily accomplished if I stay here."

Following him, Blythe told him sweetly, "Please don't be shy. Make yourself at home." She watched him as he carefully hung her cape in the bathroom to dry.

He smiled dangerously. "That's exactly what I intend doing." Leaning against the doorjamb, he added, "I don't have enough money to stay in a hotel."

"Oh, no you don't," Blythe retorted. "I won't be taken in by a sob story. I've heard the best from the best—my brother Harlan, when he went through *his* ski-bum stage. My parents despaired at first and cut off his allowance, but he's since become a respectable executive. You should emulate his example. You're certainly intelligent enough and healthy enough to get a job that will pay for little things like rent."

Cad smiled again, with that flash of white teeth that was almost incandescent, and he left the bathroom, heading for the kitchen. Opening her mouth to speak, Blythe closed it again when she realized that he was deftly preparing a mouth-watering ham and cheese omelet.

She leaned against the kitchen door, watching his quick, expert motions with irritation. Cad gave her another disarming grin before breaking the silence.

"I distinctly remember you telling me that the thing you liked best about me was that I was a real person, with no need to trod over others on my way to a fortune. I wouldn't want to reverse your good opinion of me."

Inhaling the delicious fragrances of the kitchen, Blythe felt her mouth begin to water and wondered how she could be so hungry after eating such a big dinner with Justin. "My opinion of you will not be irreversibly damaged if you earn enough money for incidentals such as food, rent, and transportation," she said dryly. "That won't make you corrupt in my book."

As he expertly folded the luscious-looking omelet, Cad said, "But at the moment I have no money whatsoever. And I need a place to stay until I can line up a job. I've pulled a muscle, and I won't be able to compete for a couple of weeks." Meeting her gaze, he grinned again. "I certainly wouldn't mind putting you up if our situations were reversed. If I had a place, that is."

Lips pursed, eyes narrowed, Blythe marched over to her purse and extracted several bills. "Here, take this money and stay in a hotel. You can pay me back when you get a job."

Cad shut off the burner on which he'd been cooking the omelet and turned to face her, his silhouette large and powerful against the predominantly white kitchen. His expression was horrified.

"I can't accept money from a woman. I'm not that kind of man."

Blythe's fingers clenched and unclenched around the bills, but she bit back the caustic retort that rose to her lips.

Smiling innocently, Cad said, "I'd be willing to work for my room and board." At her raised eyebrows, he added modestly, "By cooking and cleaning. You have a job, and apparently you work pretty late."

At Blythe's incensed expression, he explained mildly, "Mrs. Hooper told me that you very often come in quite late. You must be very tired at the end of the day. I'd be willing to have a hot meal ready for you when you come home."

At the prospect of having a live-in housekeeper-cook, Blythe's eyes shone like the jewels of King Solomon's mines. But she refused to give in to temptation.

Cad, however, had evidently noticed the bonfire in her eyes. He promised her, "I'll be a perfect gentleman. No hanky-panky, no passes. I'll just provide delicious cooking and meticulous housekeeping."

Feeling the ruins of her opposition begin to crumble inside her, Blythe attempted to speak casually. "And just how long do you foresee needing room and board?"

"A week should just about do it," he told her cheerfully.

She didn't like the gleam in his eyes, but since she counted on spending almost every available moment at the institute, his staying should not pose too much of a problem. As her stomach rumbled, she realized wryly that he was trying to get to her heart through her stomach. But, oh, the bliss of being able to work late and come home to an expertly prepared meal and a house that didn't look as if a hurricane had just swept through it.

"You can sleep on the couch. It folds out into a bed," she told him abruptly, breaking down completely at the sight of the tempting omelet he was placing in front of her.

She sat down, belatedly remembering to ask if he

wanted to eat also. But he remained standing, his tight, lean buttocks supported against the sink, and told her, "You go ahead. I fixed myself something earlier."

She was about to chide him for making himself so much at home in her kitchen, but decided to save her energy for the mouth-watering ham and cheese omelet. After all, he had cooked her supper, too, so he was earning his keep.

Cad let her eat half of the fluffy, heavenly creation before he asked, "By the way, who was that man who brought you home and kissed you in his car? The leavetaking seemed rather long."

She coughed, then tried to guide her food down the proper channels before attempting to speak. Smiling at him, she told him in a honeyed voice, "That's none of your business."

Cad frowned, his casual attitude vanishing. Blythe finished the rest of her omelet, not leaving a mouthful, and gave her compliments to the chef. "Delicious. If you can cook other things this well, the week will pass swiftly." Before he could answer, she added, "I'll get you a pillow and blanket."

As she left the kitchen to get his bedding, her mood was immensely buoyed when she saw out of the corner of her eye that Cad was still frowning at her unenlightening answer to his question about Justin.

A loud, masculine humming nearly caused Blythe to fall out of bed the following morning. She staggered about the room, looking simultaneously for cover and a weapon.

Then the events of the previous night came flooding back, and she sank onto the side of the bed, her ready-to-fight muscles relaxing.

It was quite obvious she'd grown unused to having a man around.

The wonderful aroma of coffee induced her to finish her shower in record time. Because the temperature had fallen below zero, Blythe decided to wear slacks to work. She took a dark gray woolen pants suit and a long-sleeved maroon blouse from the closet.

As she followed the almost palpable fragrance through the living room on her way to the kitchen, Blythe noticed that Cad had already put the convertible couch back together and neatly folded the bedding.

He was standing shirtless and barefoot at the counter, his powerful chest hypnotizing her as she paused uncertainly in the doorway. She'd never seen Cad in any state of undress at Indian Cove, and although she had been able to guess from the close-fitting sweaters he wore, and from her own touch, that Cad was muscular, she was unprepared for the exquisitely fluid male symmetry she encountered. His muscles seemed to glisten with health and power under that bronzed skin, and his belly, above the low-riding jeans, was a network of wiry sinew only lightly covered by a golden mist. Her fascinated gaze remained riveted on his lean hips and trim waist, and she felt an overpowering urge to run her hands through the fair hair that covered his chest and disappeared enticingly into the low-waisted, faded jeans.

"Ready to eat?"

Blythe guiltily raised her eyes from the wonderful,

intimate fit of those jeans, and met his gaze. It was full of deviltry and flooded with awareness.

This would not do. Cad had promised to behave, and while technically keeping his word, he nonetheless incited her to errant, hungry imaginings.

She cleared her throat. "Smells good." She sat down and noticed that he had made only one portion. "Aren't you going to have some pancakes and bacon, too?"

"Later. I just wanted to make sure you had time to catch the bus to work."

She added maple syrup to the heavenly breakfast and bit into a buttermilk pancake. "What do you mean? I drive to—" Then, realizing he'd seen Justin drop her off last night, she explained, "I normally drive to work, but a colleague whom I had dinner with last night gave me a ride home. He's going to pick me up this morning and drive me to the restaurant after work to pick up my car."

A slight frown marred Cad's features, but it was quickly gone. "Why don't you give me your keys? I'll pick your car up for you. That way you won't have to drive home tonight—you can get a lift from one of your colleagues, right? It hasn't stopped snowing, and the weather report said we'll be getting winds of forty or fifty miles an hour by this evening."

She hesitated. What he said made sense, but she wasn't sure if he...

He cut into her thoughts. "We're going to need some more groceries. Minnesota and Colorado are buried in snow. We don't want to be caught without supplies if the weather takes a turn for the worse, do we?"

She tried not to think how much worse the storm could get. It seemed that the weather everywhere had worsened in the past few years.

"All right. I'll give you the keys and leave you some grocery money. Buy what you think we need."

She attacked the rest of her meal with enthusiasm, and was just finishing her last bite of bacon when she felt Cad's eyes on her.

"Anything wrong?"

He shook his head. "Nope. It's just a joy to watch you eat."

She immediately felt flustered, and choked on her orange juice. "Yes, well, I hope you'll join me for supper tomorrow."

She left the kitchen a bit self-consciously, not used to leaving dishes in the sink for someone else to wash.

But Cad said as he followed her out, "Don't worry about the cleanup. That's my job, remember? I'll take care of the dishes."

His amusement did not sit well with her. She'd never been keen on housework, and not just because she'd grown up with servants in a mansion. She had found household chores boring, although that had changed when she and Lucas had begun sharing chores. Suddenly, dishes and dusting and vacuuming had not been so tiresome when they had done them together amid much clowning and fooling around, or when they carried on quiet, intimate conversations while doing the chores.

Blythe checked her watch and saw that Justin would be downstairs any minute. Cad helped her on with her cape and asked, "What time shall I have dinner ready?"

She looked at him, bemused. She'd heard those words often enough from the cook at her parents' home when she questioned Penelope Bedford as she left for one of her political or charity drives. But it was still quite strange to hear the inquiry in her own home, particularly as Lucas had not cooked well, and Blythe had made most of the meals for the two of them.

Battling her discomfiture, she said casually, "Sevenish would be fine."

At the grin on his delectable lips, Blythe abandoned her pose and said, "Oh, hell. You know this isn't easy for me. Heaven knows I'm all for equality and reversal of roles, but it does take a bit of getting used to, doesn't it? I mean, I wouldn't want to . . ." She paused, wanting to say "hurt your feelings," but not knowing if that would give inadvertent offense, too.

"Offend me?" he said, his eyes liquid gold with amusement. "You won't. My feelings are not easily injured, and I'm quite secure in my identity as a man. I don't think it demeans a man to cook and clean for a woman he . . . likes, and is grateful to, do you? It certainly hasn't demeaned the women who have been doing it for centuries."

She sighed in relief. "Yes, well, I believe that. But one never knows how to deal with—" Again she stopped herself, and Cad laughingly completed the sentence for her.

"Fragile male egos? Don't worry, my ego's intact. At least for now."

She smiled, knowing what he was referring to, but if this morning was any indication of what was to come in the next few days, she felt quite happy and lucky to have him around.

She walked to the door and told him, "See you tonight." Then she turned quickly before Cad could see in her eyes just how pleasant the thought was to her.

CHAPTER NINE

THE ARRANGEMENT WORKED quite well over the next few days—at least in Blythe's view. Cad, however, seemed to resent her coming home so late, and then bringing paperwork home with her.

Three nights later, as Blythe was relaxing with a Bacardi on the rocks, her papers spread on her lap, the TV droning on with a mindless sitcom, Cad sat on the other end of the couch and asked, "Don't you ever quit? You work twelve hours a day and then come home and put in some more time. You're getting unbecomingly skinny."

She looked up from her correspondence. "How's your job hunt coming along?"

Her pointed question did not faze him. "I might have something lined up."

This time her gaze stayed on his face. "Congratulations! That means you should be leaving soon."

He didn't share her happiness. "Are you that eager to get rid of me?"

She looked down at the papers; the fine black print seemed only a blur. No, of course she wouldn't be happy to see him go. She'd never really believed he was so destitute that he had to depend on temporary jobs. Cad did not seem the type of man who would let himself be buffeted by the winds of chance. Perhaps he'd invested unwisely, and the venture had not paid off. Maybe he'd fallen temporarily into debt.

But even that did not seem probable. She had been furious when he'd invaded her house, but the anger had left her when she'd realized that she had indeed missed Cad. The fact that he could cook and keep her house as neat as a military school had been an added benefit.

She didn't have to answer him, because he didn't give her a chance. "Dammit, Sky Eyes! Leave your blasted work for a minute."

She looked up, startled, in time to see him get up and bend to pull her to her feet. "I've behaved, but you'd try the patience of a saint. I'm tired of waiting for you, and having you come in later each night."

Blythe stared at him, aware all of a sudden that she *had* been doing that. Avoidance tactics of the highest order.

"You've got a choice, Cad, if you don't like staying here. I didn't invite you."

Her words sounded cold, hostile. But she didn't like being handled this way.

"Didn't you, Sky Eyes? We've been wanting each other since we first met, only you're too stubborn or proud or scared to admit it. I don't know which, but I've given you plenty of time."

Trying to loosen his grip on her arms, she asked, "Plenty of time for what, Cad? Are you really broke, or was this all a trick to get me into bed with you?"

"I don't need to use tricks," he told her arrogantly. "And after being here with you for a few days, seeing you each morning when you get up with that peach-rose flush on your face, your eyes all innocent and your hair tousled about your shoulders like flames . . ." His hands left her arms and dropped to her waist. "We might as well be married, Sky Eyes."

She pushed against his chest. "But we're not. And you'd better not forget it. Marriage means love and commitment, and what you feel for me is purely phys-ical."

"And you're hiding behind your work." One of his hands went to her head, dissolving the tight knot at the back of her head. The other lowered to the small of her back, pinning her hips to his.

He raked fingers through her silken hair and whis-pered as he ground his loins into hers, "Can you tell me you don't want me as much as I want you, Blythe? Your husband is dead, for heaven's sake. We're alive, remember?"

If her hands had been free instead of pinned against his chest, she'd have socked him. Cad read her look and loosened his hold on her.

"Go ahead. Hit me. At least I'll know you're the blue-eyed nymph who inhabited the forest and my heart for a few precious hours—and not an over-worked robot."

She stood motionless in the circle of his arms, and finally Cad stepped back, freeing her completely. "I guess it's worse than I thought. I'm sorry, Sky Eyes, for breaking my word. I got carried away with the domestic scene." He headed for the closet where his carryall and parka were stowed. "I'll clear out right now."

He picked up the bag and threw his coat over his shoulder, not even taking the time to retrieve his shaving kit.

"Cad, wait," she called out as he reached the door.

He turned, a mocking smile on his handsome—and by now painfully familiar—face. "Don't worry, Sky Eyes. I always pay my debts. I'll replace all the food I ate, and I'll pay my share of the rent."

She took a step toward him and stopped. She didn't want him to leave like this—she was afraid she'd never see him again—but there was a limit to how much of a commitment she could make. Her mind was a jumble of memories, images, thoughts, and feelings that precluded any reasonable decision. Save one: She wanted him to stay. Suddenly, she couldn't bear to see him go.

"Please, Cad. Don't leave." She kept her voice low to hide its revealing tremor. "You said you had a job prospect. Stay until it comes through, at least. When you're sure you've got something lined up, then you can leave."

He waited by the door, his gaze steady on hers, his every muscle unmoving. "Are you unwilling to give up my cooking? Or my excellent cleaning skills?"

She shrugged, not wanting to put her true feelings into words. "We made a pact, didn't we? You'd cook and help out until you found a job. I thought you were a man of your word."

His eyes searched hers, and he appeared satisfied at what he saw there. Blythe emitted a sigh of relief when he turned and came into the room again. She couldn't have said more than she had.

He set down his bag, telling her, "You're right. We made an agreement, and I'm a man of my word. I'll stay until I get that job." He came closer and held out his hand. "Shall we shake on it?"

Blythe smiled and shook his hand firmly. "What are we having for breakfast tomorrow?"

When she went to bed that night, she could still hear echoes of his deep chuckles reaching to entwine themselves about her heart.

"I'm home," she announced the following afternoon as she came into the apartment. She could smell appetizing aromas spreading their savory tendrils into the living room, and she was glad she had decided to leave the office at five o'clock for once.

"In the kitchen."

Blythe followed the deep, dusky voice and the aroma into the kitchen.

Cad was standing watch by the oven, and Blythe let herself enjoy the view of his athletic body in tight, worn jeans and a thick woolen shirt that hugged his muscular upper torso in loving detail.

"What happened?" He spoke casually. "Did an

earthquake hit the office? Or did you get fired?"

He turned to look at her, and his eyes warmed into a whiskey-gold, raising the inner temperature of her body to match that of the oven.

"Neither of the above," she answered, taking off her cape and jacket, finding the sudden heat oppressive. Cad's eyes slid appreciatively over her black skirt and black and royal blue silk blouse. "I skipped lunch today, so that I could gorge myself on your delicious cooking when I got home."

"Well, I'm flattered," he said, leaning his long, muscular body against the counter. "But you shouldn't skip meals. Your bones are beginning to show."

"You should write poetry," she told him wryly as she approached the oven to open the door and take a peek. "You really know how to turn a girl's head."

But Cad checked her progress by moving suddenly in front of her with one almost imperceptible maneuver. "Is there something you need?"

Her eyes went past him to the shiny white oven, but Cad would not budge. She sighed. "You have no mercy."

He moved to the refrigerator to take out her drink. "Drown your sorrows in one of these."

Blythe stole one more glance at the dinner cooking so mysteriously, and gave up. Sitting down at the table, she began to take off her high-heeled boots. When the right boot gave her a problem, Cad came over to help her, whisking it off with one deft movement.

"Any luck with your job hunting?"

"I think so," he said noncommittally. Looking

straight into her eyes as he straightened, he asked,
"By the way, where do you work? I might drop over
tomorrow and take you out to lunch."

Blythe smiled. She had not yet told him about her
job. Esther Hooper had not explained what Blythe
did, and Blythe had enlisted her landlady's help in
keeping the location of her job a secret from him.
After what he'd told her of Alessandra, she wasn't
sure how he'd react to her involvement with the institute.

"What's for dinner?" she asked, evading his question with her own.

He grinned and went to the refrigerator to take out
a quart of milk. He peeled and sliced some bananas,
put them and a few spices in a bowl with some milk,
and carried the bowl toward the kitchen gadgets that
stood in one corner of the counter. Blythe watched
with interest.

After pouring the concoction into the blender, he
peeled more bananas and put them into the blender
whole. He set the speed and pressed the button at the
same moment that Blythe remembered that she'd never
gotten the darn blender fixed.

"Cad!"

Her cry rent the small kitchen, and bedlam broke
loose.

She ran forward in time to see the cover of the
blender lift off like a rocket as the contents exploded.
A banana headed straight for Cad's eye, and the creamy
liquid flew in all directions.

The industrial-size blender kept revolving with ferocious fury, splattering the last of its contents into a

stunned Cad and a horrified Blythe. The undissolved lumps of banana became dangerous missiles, and both Cad and Blythe ducked when two more flew out toward them.

Blasting into mobility, Cad sprinted forward just in time to prevent the blender from overturning. One last chunk of banana, obviously stuck on the helix, freed itself and zoomed toward them. Blythe automatically swatted at it and felt it squish in her hand.

Keeping one broad hand on the blender for good measure, Cad half turned and asked, "You called, madam?"

The breath Blythe had been retaining blasted painfully through her nose and mouth as she registered Cad's appearance. He was covered from face to thigh by liquid and bananas, and one bite-sized piece of fruit had adhered to the end of his arrogant nose. Unbidden, laughter bubbled and rose from deep within her, and Blythe could not hold it back.

Letting the squashed banana in her palm slither to the floor, she raised both hands to her mouth to stifle her throat-hurting glee. She saw Cad's eyes darken, his profound control shaken. Anger and disgust warred for supremacy on his features, and that only made Blythe's mirth all the stronger. Strong, silent shudders racked her as she covered her mouth with her hands lest laughter escape her, and tears began to gather in her eyes.

"Are you choking, Miss Blythe?" Cad asked, adopting the supercilious tone of a butler.

She shook her head. "No." As she spoke, the first of many chuckles triumphantly emerged from her throat. Now she had as much chance of repressing her laughter as she had of turning back the tide.

Cad calmly tore the plug from the wall and turned to her once more, wiping his hands on the seat of his pants. Since he'd been facing the blender when disaster struck, his tight buttocks were one of the few unspattered sections of his substantial frame.

Then he began to advance lazily toward her.

Her eyes widening, Blythe held her hands out in front of her and began to back away awkwardly, bent over with laughter.

"Cad . . ." she got out between choking chuckles and great gulps of air. "I'm not laughing *at* . . . you . . . I'm . . . laughing . . . with you."

He continued to approach her. Blythe backed around the kitchen table and felt another paroxysm of hilarity shake her when Cad looked for a handkerchief in his back pocket, found none, and wiped a clod of mashed banana off his eye and nose with the back of his hand.

He grinned. Blythe was not reassured.

"You had it all planned, didn't you?" he accused her. "Maybe to try to pay me back for the things I said yesterday. You just sat there, all prim and proper, calmly waiting for all hell to break loose."

He had it all wrong, she thought, her laughter diminishing somewhat at his interpretation of the incident. She shook her head, feeling helpless hiccups start to erupt, and tried to talk. "No, Cad . . . you're wr-wrong. R-really . . . I didn't pl-plan this . . ."

He didn't believe her. She tried to lunge toward the door, but he was quicker and was there in an instant, blocking her exit.

She retreated again. He advanced.

Her chuckles had been transformed into giggling hiccups. Blythe was running out of breath, and space. She hadn't laughed this hard in . . . in as long as she could remember.

She tried to get a grip on herself as Cad closed in for the kill, but resolve and restraint went out the window when Cad slipped on a banana peel that had been blown to the floor in the force of the gadget explosion.

"Oh, Cad . . ." She laughed anew and unwisely, pointing to the slippery peel.

He advanced the last two steps, pinning her against the kitchen sink. "I'm glad you're enjoying yourself so much, Sky Eyes, because now it's my turn."

Grabbing her by the waist and picking her up with one arm despite her attempt to struggle, kicking weakly, he carried her to the vanquished blender. Then he stuck his hand inside the container to scoop out the remaining sticky liquid, and set her down between himself and the refrigerator, holding his hand up like the ultimate weapon.

"Now apologize," he ordered, stilling her wriggling by squeezing her legs between his own.

"N-never . . ." she got out between hiccups. "It—it was all an acci-accident . . ."

His fingers approached her face. "And you dare to continue to laugh?"

"C-can't st-stop," she told him, lifting a weakened hand and attempting to stop his descending arm.

His hand made contact, rubbing the creamy substance on her nose and cheeks and chin. "How do you like it?" he growled, and then- he was brushing his fingers on her mouth before his lips fell upon hers, cutting off her protests.

She could taste the banana and spices and his own natural flavor as his lips parted hers and his tongue thrust inside. He chewed on her lower lip before soothing it with his tongue in rolling combat, and then attacked the soft insides of her cheeks.

She moaned, and the sound was intermixed with diminishing hiccups. His tongue seemed to absorb the vibration, and he delved farther into her mouth, his contact searing, voracious. But when he began to withdraw his tongue, she captured it, retaining it in her hot cavity and nibbling it with her teeth.

This time it was Cad who groaned, and his legs parted to let her slide to the floor. She felt the coolness of the refrigerator against her back and the scorching heat of his body against her breasts and stomach. The occasional hiccup was banished as his hand left her face and descended to her silk blouse, popping the covered buttons open, while the hand at her waist circled it to rest on her hip and massage it.

Blythe lifted arms heavy with weakness and entwined them about his neck, feeling dizzy from the laughter, dazed from the sensual waves buffeting her. His mouth suddenly lifted from hers, and she swallowed precious air before it was chased away by Cad's hand closing about her swollen breast and his erotic tickling of her nose.

Her hiccups having been most effectively, sensually chased away, Blythe murmured, "Cad, it *was* an accident." His lips nibbled on hers for a moment,

interrupting her and destroying her train of thought.
She tried to move her head a bit in an effort to recall
what she'd been saying, and his lips ceased their stalk-
ing of her face and plundered the long, graceful curve
of her neck.

She tried again. "Cad, I had just remembered that
the blender needed fixing when I yelled." Her voice
was soft and trembling, echoing the shivers that were
inundating her body as his lips closed about the soft
skin of her throat. "Cad. Cad—"

She desisted. It was no use trying to explain. Her
thoughts were not rational anymore.

He lifted his head to look down at her and said, "I
need a lot of convincing. I still say you planned it,"
and then his mouth began its sensual attack again, a
series of prolonged, sucking kisses that sent a long
shudder from her neck to her toes, curling them and
leaving her limp.

His arms went immediately about her, pulling her
away from the refrigerator. "Are you cold?" he asked
in husky concern.

About to say no, Blythe disregarded all her self-
control and long-embedded discipline and nodded yes.
Cad lifted her into his arms and sat down near the
table, with her on his lap.

"I'm sorry," he said contritely, his gaze heavy-
lidded with passion as he dropped sweet, soft kisses
on her eyelids. "You are the most delectable thing in
this kitchen, and I got carried away. I would like to
make love to you here, on the kitchen floor, on the
table, on the couch, standing up..." She flushed inside and out at the sexual force in his words and at

the aroused male body that was hard against hers. "But I should have thought of you first." He placed a kiss on her nose. "Forgive me?"

She laced her arms about his neck and said quietly, "There's nothing to forgive. I wouldn't care where we made love, either." At the sudden flare of renewed desire in his eyes, she raised a hand and placed it on his lips. "What concerns me is *when*, Cad. I—I'm just not sure..."

At the moment, she didn't know what she wanted most. She was torn in two—one part of her, the sensible, cautious part, telling her she should wait, she should have control over her actions; the other, newly born and impetuous, telling her it would be a natural, beautiful thing to make love with Cad right now.

It would have been easier to leave the decision up to him. The flames of arousal were simmering uneasily, potently, within her. He could have fanned them into full, flaring passion with little effort. But this was her decision, and it would be foolish and unfair to expect Cad to seduce her into acquiescence.

He didn't.

With what she knew was a great effort, he let her go and got up. "Well, Sky Eyes, the most stupid promise I've ever made in my life was to tell you I wouldn't push you. I won't break my word, though." He fingered a heavy lock of hair that had escaped from her tight chignon and now tumbled over her ivory breast. Her breasts ached under the force of his heated appraisal, and the nipples pouted, an angry, aroused red.

His hands trembled as he pulled the open front of her blouse together, and then he was moving away stiffly, going to check on the meal in the oven. "Almost ready," he announced throatily.

Blythe felt guilty at his obvious torment. But she told herself that her body was on fire, too, and it was best if they both extinguished the flames for a while. Their propinquity made such encounters as they'd just had almost inevitable. But just because something was normal and natural didn't mean it was to be mindlessly indulged in.

She went to stand by Cad and put her hand lightly on his shoulder. He tensed, and without turning around said, "Please, Blythe. I'd appreciate it if you wouldn't touch me right now. I'm about to burst."

Blythe dropped her hand hurriedly, as if she'd been scorched. Which she had, she admitted ruefully. "Cad, I'm sorry . . ." Then she decided to leave that subject alone and said instead, "Cad, I didn't do it on purpose . . ."

He turned his head, then, and looked at her. "Blythe, if you're trying to tell me you're not a tease, it's not necessary. I asked for what I got."

Her face reddened, and she bit her lower lip, "Oh, well, I'm glad you feel that way." She took a grip on herself, angry at her lack of composure. "I meant about the bananas, though," she told him. And her hastily buried laughter began to bubble inside her again. Trying to keep a straight face, she added, "I didn't plan the banana explosion."

His lips curved into a reluctant grin. "I know that, too—now. Before, I was blinded by passion. And your laughter is an aphrodisiac for me, Blythe. I love to see you laugh. Your eyes shine like sapphires."

"Hm. It's going to be hard to be around you, then, isn't it? I hope that doesn't mean I have to stop laughing altogether. Because it certainly will be difficult not to laugh every time I remember your expression, or how you were covered with—" Cad took a step toward her, and she backed away hastily toward the door—"bananas, and how you slipped on one of them." She ran into the bedroom to change, laughter already taking a strong hold of her, as she remembered how for once Cad's monumental composure had been shattered.

As she lay in bed four hours later, Blythe found it hard to fall asleep. She rolled to her side to look out the window and watch the snow gently carpet the already white branches of a tree that bent under the force of the wind and its white weight.

She had been happy in the small, second-story apartment. It had been convenient—close to work and easy to clean. There was not that much to clean, at that, not like the apartment she'd shared with Lucas. She had wanted to resist the painful memories that had assailed her each night as she tried to sleep, the spot on the right side of the bed empty.

But now, new memories had been created. Through the window, she saw a branch laden with snow bow under the weight, releasing its crystalline covering. She felt as if she, too, were being buffeted by change, and by the force of her own emotions. She had wanted so to inhabit a quiet, emotionally even world for a while, a stretch of time when she could finish healing, and not go through any more upheavals.

But that hope, that plan, had been scratched when she met Cad. He was a whirlwind that had blown down her carefully constructed foundations. He'd taken her by storm, and now no evenness, no sense of balance, was possible. She was fighting too powerful an undercurrent; in addition to Cad's feelings for her, she was battling her own attraction for him.

It had been hard for her to air her misgivings. It would have been so much easier to let herself be carried along by the tide. But just as she felt a new emptiness now, lying alone in bed, she hated to think how she would feel when Cad left. For he was bound to go sometime. He'd given no indication of wanting to settle down, and she certainly didn't want to become utterly vulnerable only to lose him. The grief of loss had been too raw the first time.

Yet she knew Cad was not using her. She was sure he had followed her just to be with her; someone of his impulsive nature would not take kindly to waiting three months. He'd made clear how much he wanted her—had demonstrated it very eloquently tonight.

She was afraid to get involved again. And yet, did it really matter if Cad was not serious? She herself certainly wasn't ready to contemplate another marriage, so what would be the harm in getting involved with Cad?

As she turned impatiently onto her back, she told herself she knew the answer to that: too deep an attachment to Cad.

She pictured him in the living room, his big frame

contorted or overflowing in the couch. She beat her fist into the pillow at the realization of how much she wanted to make love with Cad. She was ready to use any rationalization to go out there and throw herself into his arms and make wild, passionate love to him.

But fear held her back. Fear that once in his arms, she'd never want to leave them...

CHAPTER TEN

"WELL, I THINK that's enough for one day," Blythe announced the following evening. She put down the disbursement ledger she'd been studying and smiled at Cad. "I'm going to bed."

Cad nodded, his expression brooding. Dinner tonight had been somewhat uncomfortable; it had been the first time Blythe had felt ill at ease with Cad. Sexual tension was brittle between them, and she knew it was costing Cad just as much as it was her to try to keep things on an even keel.

Before heading for the bedroom, she turned and said, "Tonight's dinner was magnificent. Fish yesterday, Cornish hens today. You're spoiling me, Cad. I don't know what I'll do when you're not..." The words died in her throat, and she saw Cad's eyes darken in response to what she'd left unsaid.

Standing up, he stretched, the muscles almost bursting the seams of his old, clingy T-shirt. "I'll turn in, too. And don't worry about the budget. I've learned just where to shop, and we'll be eating meat loaf for the next couple dinners to make up for the feasts these past two days."

"Sounds fair," she told him, keeping her eyes on his face where they wouldn't be able to transmit dangerous messages to her brain. "See you in the morning, then."

She felt strange going into the bedroom without a good-night kiss. After all, they were more than casual acquaintants. But it would be playing with fire if they followed their instincts, and so they dispensed with tender greetings and bade each other stiff good nights.

She'd taken a quick shower when she got home, so now she undressed, put on a lilac nightgown, and got into bed.

But like the night before, she had trouble falling asleep. She turned and squirmed, and squirmed and turned some more, until she could no longer stand the restlessness. Sitting up in bed, Blythe took a book out of the built-in bookcase in the headboard of her bed, and tried to concentrate on it. When *Les Misérables* by Victor Hugo could not hold her attention, despite the fact that it was one of her favorites, she faced the fact that she was not in a mood for reading.

Her glance sneaked to the closed bedroom door, and she immediately forced herself to turn off the reading lamp and slide back down in bed.

But another half-hour of useless, nerve-racking tossing and turning told her she wouldn't get to sleep tonight until she did something. No, not *that* something, she told her suggestive mind.

Grabbing the robe that matched the lace and satin nightgown she'd bought for her honeymoon with Lucas, Blythe tiptoed to the door, opened it softly, and tiptoed out.

She waited for a minute to accustom herself to the darkness of the living room, and then made her way slowly and silently to the kitchen. Once there, she felt her way around the refrigerator. She really had a taste for hot cocoa, but didn't want to risk waking up Cad. So, after pouring herself a glass of milk by the light of the refrigerator, she closed the door softly and took a thirsty sip.

"Blythe, are you all right?"

The voice behind her caught her just as she was about to turn around. Unnerved, she yelped, the tall, cold glass flying out of her hand and its contents splashing over Cad's broad, bare chest.

Cad jumped back instinctively as the icy liquid made contact, and he swore under his breath.

"I can see you're all right," he said as Blythe heard his ineffectual slapping away of the milk on his chest. She tried to get around him to turn on the light at the other end of the kitchen, but misjudged in the Stygian darkness and bumped into Cad's chest. His arms closed about her.

"Stand still. There may be broken glass on the floor."

He picked her up, moved sideways and then a few

steps ahead until he bumped into the kitchen table.
Gingerly, he maneuvered his way around until he
found a kitchen chair and sat down, with Blythe in
his lap.

"The most interesting things do happen to us in the
kitchen, don't they?" he told her huskily as he shifted
her more comfortably onto his hard thighs.

Blythe chuckled. "I'm sorry, Cad. I didn't want to
wake you up. I didn't turn on the kitchen light, because it spills out into the living room."

"You didn't wake me. I wasn't asleep. But I thought
you might be feeling sick, or coming down with something." Passing one hand over his sticky chest, he said
wryly, "Instead, I seem to be the one who came down
with a nice bath."

Another laugh escaped her, and she said, "You do
seem to be accident-prone, don't you, Cad?"

"Next time I'll turn on all lights, hire a marching
band, and announce over the loudspeaker that I'm
approaching." He passed his hand over his chest again,
his elbow brushing against her breast, and said, "Damn,
this stuff is sticky."

"It's supposed to be good for your skin. Milk and
egg are said to do wonders for you."

His voice lowered. "You know what would do
wonders for *me*." His mouth found hers unerringly in
the dark, and he asked her, "Want to be good for my
skin, not to mention all those other aching, swollen
parts of me?"

She felt him against her hip, giving substance to
his words. She caught her breath as his right hand slid
over her thigh, skimmed lightly over her stomach,

and paused just a fraction of an inch beneath the lower curve of her breast.

"Well, Sky Eyes? Yes or no?"

The silence that followed was fraught with tension. His lips were still hovering over hers, his breathing even, his heartbeat strong, his body immobile. The next move was up to her.

Apparently, he took her silence for a denial, because he sighed and began to get up. "Well, the sticky bath was worth it since I got to hold you for a few minutes. Only next time try to make it scotch, okay? It evaporates faster."

She clutched at his shoulders and said, "You're rather impatient, aren't you? I sure hope this tendency to hurry doesn't carry over into your lovemaking."

"Now, a statement like *that* can destroy a man's ego," Cad said, sitting back down and rearranging her legs so they were wrapped around his waist. "You'll eat your words before I'm through with you."

"Take your time, please," she told him, leaning forward to place a series of kisses on his throat and shoulders. "Make sure you convince me thoroughly."

He clamped one hand about her waist and grabbed her chin with the other. "I will, but you'd better stop that, Sky Eyes. I have only so much self-control left after living with you and sleeping only a few feet away from you these interminable nights." Dropping a kiss on her mouth, he told her, "We'll concentrate on you first."

And he did just that.

For the next few minutes, his mouth searched every corner, every secret of hers. His hands traveled slowly over every inch of flesh, rubbing the silken material over her skin. Her breathing was heavy, erratic; her heartbeat hammered in conjunction with the blood thundering in her veins.

"Lord, you're lovely, Blythe," he told her as his lips trailed over the upper swell of her breast, following the line of lace he found there. "Let's get you to bed."

She shook her head. Her hands were on Cad's waist, and she longed to move them along the length of his lean body, to caress and excite him. "Remember what you said about our nice experiences in this kitchen? Let's add one more."

His hands lowered to her buttocks, and he drew her closer to him. "Are you sure? You'll be more comfortable in bed."

"I don't want to be more comfortable." She gave in to her yearning and ran her hands over his shoulders, his back, down to the belt of his jeans. "I want us to join, now."

One of his hands lifted her bottom to slide the nightgown and robe up from her thighs, his fingers circling on the material so that her flesh felt tingly all over from the tickling sensation of it. He let the robe slip from her shoulders, and the nightgown bundle up around her hips, his fingers once more following the path of lace on her breasts. When his palm rubbed circles on the throbbing mounds, she felt her breast expand achingly and her nipple burn under the sensual friction.

Bending his head, he continued his excruciatingly pleasurable petting of one breast while his lips cap-

tured the aching peak of another, biting sharply through
the soft-rough material. Blythe moaned, and her head
was suddenly too heavy, too stuporous to support.
She rested her damp forehead on Cad's shoulder, and
let her hands trail tantalizing, lethargic patterns along
his spine.

Cad's sweat-sheened body tensed under her response and touch. His hands went to his belt, but
Blythe aroused herself slightly from her pleasurable
languor to stop him.

"Let me," she whispered, her fingers slow and
clumsy on the buttoned front closure.

Cad leaned back slightly to allow her easier access,
and his hands covered hers for a minute. "Are you
sure, Blythe?"

His husky, concerned tone warmed her and melted
the last of her debilitated resistance. She lowered her
head to his chest and placed a cascade of kisses on
its broad, lightly matted surface, feeling the muscles
straining under the smooth skin beneath her lips. She
said against his heart, "Very, very sure."

And she was. As she disposed of his cumbersome
buttons, she reflected that it was time. She was still
afraid, but some deep, primitive instinct urged her to
take the moment as it came.

And nothing seemed more right at the moment than
to lose herself in Cad's embrace.

When her hands found him, he gasped. His hands,
which had remained lightly on her waist and the side
of her breast, clutched her tightly. He slid her back
a fraction on his thighs, so he could gain access to
her stomach, and the red-gold mound below.

"I think you've done enough damage," he told her, removing her cool fingers from his engorged man-hood, which had come to thrusting life under her touch. "Let me repair some of it before I come into your hands."

Blythe reluctantly moved her hands to his waist, missing that vital part of him that had blossomed with her touch. During the past year, she had not experi-enced sexual longing, but it now hit her with tidal-wave force. And like the tide, it could not be turned back. Nor did she want to suppress it.

His hands quickly disposed of her gown, and then he was bringing her against his chest in a convulsive movement. Her breasts flattened against him, and her body molded itself to his. They held each other for a sweet eternity, and then he was lifting her, accom-modating her soft curves to his hard angles. She guided him in lovingly, breathlessly, dizzyingly aware of the perfect fit, the glorious harmony, of their bodies.

Cad thrust upward, and a cry escaped Blythe's parted lips as he filled her to almost unbearable full-ness. He stayed motionless within her for a timeless moment, and she clutched his shoulders, overcome by the sensations running amok in her body, and by the sense of peace that accompanied them.

Then his hands tightened on her buttocks, urging her into a smooth, easy rhythm, and Blythe showered kisses on his shoulders. One of his hands left her bottom and found its way between their bodies to cup a breast and knead it, his thumb brushing the nipple in quick, shiver-inducing motions. Blythe moaned and her kisses became tender nibbles on his flesh.

Cad moved his hips powerfully, and Blythe felt

the first of a series of overwhelming convulsions. She held on to Cad's shoulders as the world around them lost its stability and then ceased to exist. Reality was composed only of their two bodies straining toward each other, physically blending into one. She moaned helplessly under the onslaught, feeling the waves of pleasure crash and recede in her body, only to crash again under Cad's expert tutelage.

His hands massaged her bottom as they controlled her, ignoring her pleas to stop. He swallowed her cries in his mouth, his tongue delving deep inside to echo their other profound joining.

Boneless, she finally collapsed on him after the last, soul-wringing shudder. The words "I love you" were singing in her brain, and she said them silently against Cad's mouth.

He held her until the last of her spasms had stilled, and her body had once again descended to normality. He soothed her with soft murmurings, and gentle touches, and then his body was thrusting upward, sinking deeper and deeper.

Blythe welcomed him, opening herself wider, receiving him until she was brimming with the feel, touch, scent of him. He heaved into her even deeper, harder, and then faster as he strove toward his own pinnacle. Then, with one final thrust, he buried himself in her as Blythe bore down, trying to remove any physical barrier between them. His climax brought on another one of her own, fainter this time, but just as satisfying, and his cry of her name mingled with her own gasp of ecstasy as they both climbed to the stars in unison.

Blythe felt her body quiver in the slow, somnolent

descent from rapture. Her thighs, wrapped about Cad's hips, shuddered slightly. He massaged them, rubbing soft, soothing circles on them, and on her buttocks, and then he rose with her in his arms.

Lassitude stealing over her body like a sensual sedative, Blythe asked, "Where are we going?"

"To bed, Sky Eyes. To make love properly."

She circled his neck with arms that felt as if they had dissolved, and murmured, "You mean what we did just now wasn't proper? Funny, I'd have said we both reached some satisfaction."

He kissed her, hard, and said, "What we did just now was perfect... You were dynamite. But if I'm to have any energy left for the rest of the night, I need a softer resting place. My butt feels as though it's been demolished."

"Poor Cad," Blythe soothed, lowering one hand to comfort the abused part of his anatomy. Then, remembering his other statement, she asked, "The rest of the night?"

"The rest of the night," he affirmed. "I have to make up for lost time."

She yawned prodigiously. "I don't think I'll be able to stay awake."

She could feel his smile as he nuzzled her throat.

"Don't worry," he crooned. "I have foolproof, time-tested methods of torture. You won't fall asleep on me."

She tried to stifle another yawn, unsuccessfully. "If you say so..." she murmured, cuddling close to him.

But they'd already reached her bedroom, and Cad

was depositing her in the cool bed. Only half awake now, she protested vigorously. "Cad, where are you? I'm freezing. Come keep me warm."

He came toward her, and she rose on an elbow, looking incredulously at the billowing curtains and realizing he had opened the window. "Have you slipped a cog? It's glacial out there."

"But it won't be cold in here for long," he told her, throwing himself on top of her. "There, isn't that better?" he asked, lifting his upper torso from hers and running one very talented hand from her thigh to her throat, taking careful notice of strategic places in between.

She felt her languor chased away by desire, and she clasped his neck, bringing his mouth to within tantalizing millimeters of hers. "You cruel, insensitive, pitiless monster," she protested, but soon he drove all thought of even playful complaint from her mind.

Blythe felt Cad surge inside her.

"Again? This is the fourth time!"

"Who's counting?" he answered, nibbling on a tender earlobe, then tracing the spiral seashell with a velvet-rough tongue. "Besides, I told you we'd get it right..."

"And we haven't yet?" Blythe asked throatily as his tongue plunged in her ear.

"Perfection requires much practice," he whispered as he withdrew and penetrated her again with a powerful, perfect motion...

*   *   *

"You look positively radiant," Gladys chirped as Blythe tried to make an unobtrusive entrance at the institute the following morning.

Blythe groaned as she saw her secretary pick up her coffee cup and follow her into the inner office. Gossip time.

"I've never known you to be late before," Gladys blithely continued. "Sleeping in must agree with you."

Blythe gave Gladys a grimace that she hoped passed for a smile and gingerly sat in her swivel chair. All her nerve endings positively screamed, and she felt her inner thighs begin to tremble.

"By the way, Nimms called to say he can't make the appointment on Friday, either." Blythe groaned, and Gladys continued, "But he'd like you to attend a party on Saturday. He can give you fifteen minutes, then—it's your last chance before he goes to Europe on vacation."

"How generous," Blythe muttered sarcastically. She rested her head on her hand, hoping to anchor it so it wouldn't float away.

"What's the matter?" Gladys asked solicitously. "Got a headache?"

Bodyache, Blythe thought silently, and attempted another wan smile. "I'm afraid so."

"Hope you're not coming down with the flu," Gladys told her with concern. "Here, let me get you some coffee and an aspirin."

"Thanks, Glad. Maybe just some water. And you can leave the whole aspirin bottle."

When the secretary left, Blythe slunk down in her seat, trying to find relief for her supersensitive body.

She'd grown unaccustomed to lovemaking, and Cad had put her through the paces.

She straightened with an effort, and began sorting the papers piled in her in-basket.

That evening, Cad met her at the door, enfolding her in a crushing embrace.

"Please, be careful with the merchandise," Blythe exhorted him, only half humorously. "It's super-fragile."

"Sorry," Cad said, hugging her lightly. He led her to the couch. "Here, take your shoes off and put your feet up while I get you a drink."

"Not tonight, please. Maybe some tea."

His eyebrows rose wickedly. "Feeling out of sorts?"

"Just let me rest a few minutes and then *I'll* make *you* dinner tonight." His grin infuriated her, and she told him, "Don't look so smug. You put me through the wringer last night."

"Well, just between us, I'm a bit sore, too," he told her, heading for the kitchen. "You're voracious."

"*I* am?" she said indignantly as he came back into the living room. "You're no slouch."

"That's because you're a true inspiration to me." He sat beside her and put her feet in his lap, massaging them. "Any comments at work regarding the lateness of the redoubtable Ms. Bedford?"

"Yes. My secretary feared I had come down with something."

"You did, Sky Eyes. You came down with me," he said suggestively, tickling the soles of her feet.

She groaned at his double entendre. "You're terrible." When he began leaning toward her, his intentions quite clear from his expression, Blythe pushed at him. "Let me up. You're getting the night off. You get to sample my cooking tonight, and put *your* feet up for a change."

He kept coming, and she said with mingled desperation and desire, "Please, Cad. I don't think I can take any more."

"You'd be surprised what the human body can take," he murmured against her throat. "And don't worry about dinner. I'd rather have you." His hand burrowed underneath her skirt and caressed her thigh.

"You're a sadist." His other hand slipped her blouse from her skirt and she whispered, "Be gentle."

"Anyway you want it, my love," Cad said, opening the buttons with two fingers. She gazed at the gold hairs on the back of his hand, admiring his amazing dexterity with her buttons at the same time as she wondered about the meaning of his endearment.

Just then the teakettle began to whistle, and Blythe jumped, hitting Cad in the chin. "See, you're the sadist here," he pointed out, rubbing his jaw gingerly. "I'd better move to a safer spot." He buried his head in the scented valley between her breasts.

Blythe wanted to stop him, to tell him that the piercing sound of the teakettle was grating on her nerves. But as he continued his sensual magic, her brain accepted only his erotic stimuli, ignoring the intrusive noise until she felt she was insensitive to all but his touch, his musky male odor, and his mouth.

But another shrill sound encroached on their private universe, and this she could not ignore or tune out.

"The telephone, Cad."

"They'll call back," Cad said, beginning to work on her skirt. Apparently, he was able to tune out all external disturbances.

Blythe evaded his seeking mouth, and said, "Cad, it could be from my workplace."

"At this hour?" He pulled back and looked at her face. "All right, if you're that concerned, answer it this time and then we'll take it off the hook." As he reached across the couch to the small table where the phone rested and handed it to her, he said, "Bad tactical error. I should have taken the phone off the hook the minute you walked in the door."

She took the receiver from him. "Hello. Yes, Justin. What?" She sat up, and Cad moved back to give her some room, his hand going to the nape of her neck and softly massaging it. "Are you sure Timmy's gone?" she asked, barely registering that Cad's fingers slowed down. "But why would he want to run away from the institute?" As soon as she asked the question, she realized what she'd said, and saw in Cad's eyes what she'd been afraid to see. But the child who had disappeared from the institute took precedence. "Listen," she told Justin, "I'll get dressed and come out there right now. It should only take fifteen, twenty minutes." Cad's hand left the back of her neck. "Yes, tell the nurse to come in, please. I'd like to question her. That child can barely walk, and in this weather ...oh, God, Justin..." Her voice broke, and she made an effort to pull herself together. "I'll be right there."

CHAPTER ELEVEN

CAD'S FACE WAS STONY, his expression unreadable. Blythe looked for a spark of communication between them, but saw none.

She got up unsteadily, and he rose, too, waiting.

"Cad...I have to go. One of my children—the institute's children—is missing. I have—"

"That slip of the tongue was very revealing. No wonder you live for your work."

"My work is important. I'm director of the Institute for Disabled Children and—"

"You couldn't see fit to tell me? Why the big mystery? You even enlisted Esther Hooper's help, didn't you, so I wouldn't find out what you did."

Blythe's nervousness began to give way to anger.

"It's not some dark, sordid secret, Cad. *I'm* proud

of what I do. It's *you* who are prejudiced against my job, because of Alessandra..."

He stiffened, but his eyes were still unfathomable. "I didn't think you'd throw a confidence in my face."

"Oh, Cad, I'm not," Blythe said, her voice softening as she took a step toward him, wanting to touch him, to work things out between them. "But I was afraid you would react this way when I told you— exactly as you're doing now. And since you never conceded that you might have been wrong about Alessandra, since you never gave *her* the benefit of the doubt, I wanted to make sure you knew me first, before I told you about my job. I don't work at the institute for any silly social reasons, Cad, but because—"

"Why you work there is not the point right now, Blythe," he cut in again. "You deceived me, deliberately—"

"But not maliciously, Cad. I wanted to show you the institute, let you see the work we do, so that you'd understand..."

"And were you going to show me before or after I left, Blythe? Were you going to show me at all, or was our lovemaking a charming little interlude for you, to cure your loneliness? Or perhaps you just wanted to make full use of my talents while I was here—you know, in addition to my cooking, cleaning..."

She paled, and reeled as if from a blow. Cad's expression softened slightly, but his eyes remained implacable.

"I'm sorry, Blythe. That was a cheap shot. I guess

I'm even more involved with you than I'd realized,
and being deceived like this . . . well, it was a knee-
jerk reaction."

Blythe nodded, her face set. She put on her shoes
and went to get her coat. "I have to go, Cad. A little
boy's missing, and I have to help find him. If you're
interested in giving the institute—and me—a fair
chance, come see for yourself." She gave him the
address and walked to the door.

Cad didn't stop her.

Justin was already at the institute when she arrived.
He'd alerted the police, and neighbors had volunteered
to help in the search for Timmy. Justin had stayed late
at the office to grapple with some figures, and he'd
been the first to learn from the night nurse of Timmy's
disappearance. Gladys arrived a few minutes after
Blythe.

The search continued through the night, and Blythe
became more and more worried as each minute passed.
The temperature dropped below freezing as a cold
northern front moved in, and by dawn snow had begun
to fall, slowly, gently blanketing the city. The search
took on an even more frantic quality.

Blythe was surprised when a couple of private detectives came to offer their services, free of charge.
She was very thankful, and showed them a picture of
Timmy, telling them what he'd been wearing that
day—jeans, a sweater, and a Windbreaker. His pa-
jamas remained neatly folded on the bed, and the
clothes he'd worn all day were missing from the closet.

At one point, Blythe imagined she saw Cad among

the volunteers who'd come in to ask what areas they should search before going out into the cold night. But she dismissed her glimpse of Cad as her tired imaginings. She'd probably wanted to see that tall frame, that golden head, and had confused him with some other volunteer.

As the rest of the city slowly woke to snow-covered surroundings, Blythe finally received news. Timmy had been found.

Unharmed, a little scared, he had been discovered in one of the all-night lounges a few blocks away from the institute. One of the volunteer detectives had combed the area when Blythe had suggested that Timmy was smart enough to come in from the cold, and would probably seek refuge in the hall of an apartment building, or perhaps a store.

A big cheer went up when the private investigator brought Timmy in bundled up in his own coat, and Gladys cut through the ensuing commotion to say that there was still some coffee and hot chocolate left, which some thoughtful neighbors had provided for the chilled searchers.

The nurse put Timmy to bed right away, after she had determined that he was in good health. She gave the boy some hot chocolate, and he went to sleep immediately. Blythe wasn't about to interrogate the youngster, after his ordeal. Time enough tomorrow to find out why Timmy had run away.

After thanking everyone, Blythe went home with Gladys, who offered her a change of clothes that Gladys's sister, June, who was about Blythe's height, had left there. Then Blythe called Cad from Gladys's apartment—which was only five blocks from the institute—but got no answer. She tried to convince herself that he really had been one of the volunteers last night, but remembering his reaction to the phone call from Justin, she began to think that perhaps he'd left.

A cold fist seemed to envelop her heart and squeeze it at that thought, but she fought against despair. She changed quickly and refused Gladys's offer of breakfast, wanting to get back to the institute, where she could talk to Timmy as soon as he awakened.

As they drove to the office, Gladys looked at her, concerned. "You sure you're all right, Blythe? You look as if you'd lost something, not found it. Timmy's going to be all right, you know."

Blythe smiled warmly at her friend. "I guess the aftershock is settling in. I couldn't have forgiven myself if something had happened to Timmy."

"You didn't have anything to do with his running away. And it's not the first time one of the children has pulled a stunt like that."

"I know, Glad. But still, it's my responsibility. I should have noticed if Timmy was having problems—someone should have."

"Well, the nurse who used to work with him probably did. But she quit without bothering to enlighten anyone else."

Blythe nodded. "She couldn't stay any longer, Glad. You can't really blame her. She has an elderly mother to care for, and she needed more money than we could afford to pay her."

"I guess," Gladys said as she expertly parallel-parked. Patting Blythe's hand, she said, "Now, make sure you don't overdo it, boss."

Blythe gave her a quick hug and smiled. "Look who's talking." Once inside, they went their separate ways, and Blythe headed for the clinic. "I'm going to check on Timmy. I'll join you in the office later."

"Hi, Timmy."

Timmy smiled up at her a bit timidly. In his seven-year-old eyes was a knowledge of pain and suffering that no child should possess.

Blythe swallowed past the burning lump in her throat as she sat on the edge of the bed, her hand going to Timmy's forehead to brush a fair lock of silky hair away. "You gave us quite a scare, young man," she told him softly, wanting him to know that what he did was wrong, but not wanting him to think he was any less loved because of it.

"Are you—are you..." The little mouth moved painfully, and Timmy's words emerged in a frightened squeak. "Are you going to send me away?"

"Send you away?" Blythe asked. "Whatever gave you that idea?"

"Matthew said that you hadn't been to see me lately because you were going to send me away. He said I must have been a bad boy because my—my—" Timmy stumbled over a sob, but bravely tried to choke it back. "Be-because my parents and sister died."

Blythe closed her eyes. This was what she was faced with—children of all ages with various physical disabilities and emotional problems, all of them under one roof. Many of them had no place else to go, either because they were orphans or because the fathers had abandoned the families and the mothers could not support their children, particularly those who required special care. Timmy had come from a well-to-do family, but the surviving aunt and uncle had not wanted to be—and she remembered their exact words—"bogged down with a child who required special treatment." They already had three healthy boys of their own.

She smoothed Timmy's forehead, trying to fight back the tears that burned in her throat and threatened to spill over. Matthew also came from a family that could have supported him, but had chosen not to. And she couldn't censure Matthew's bitterness or condemn him too harshly when he struck out blindly at Timmy because of his own pain.

Adults, she knew, were capable of much subtler and more refined cruelties. And with a lot less reason.

But now she had Timmy's pain to deal with.

When she felt she could control her wobbly voice, Blythe told him, "Timmy, I want to get one thing clear. Right now. Then we won't talk about this ever again. Okay?"

Timmy nodded, his hazel eyes huge in his thin, pale face. "Do you trust me?" she asked. He nodded again. "Then you have to believe me when I say that I will *never* send you away. No matter how many times you run away. Or how badly you behave. Okay?"

His throat worked feverishly. "Okay."

"But I'm not pleased at what you did last night. You had us very worried, and a lot of people didn't get to bed at all, because they were combing the city in the freezing weather to try to find you. And I'm very, very disappointed in you."

Timmy gulped, but Blythe forced herself to continue. "I may not like your behavior—I may be furious about it, as I am right now—but I'll never ever stop loving you. It's your behavior I don't like. Not you." She took his hand and stroked it. "Do you understand what I'm telling you?"

Blythe got another nod, this time more vigorous. Apparently, Timmy's greatest fear had been that he'd be sent away. Now that this wasn't likely to happen, he was ready for anything.

"Because this is the first time you've pulled such a stunt, your punishment won't be severe. But there won't be a next time, will there?"

Timmy shook his head so that his fair curls bounced against the pillow, his expression solemn. "For your punishment this time," Blythe told him neutrally, "you'll skip dessert for the next three days."

She could feel all the tenseness dissolve from Timmy's slight body, and she smiled inwardly. She knew Timmy thought he was getting off scot-free. She'd chosen his punishment deliberately, since unlike most children, Timmy didn't particularly like sweets. But the boy would not be aware that she knew his preferences. And the other children, who loved their desserts, would see that Timmy had been disciplined for his wrongdoing.

She leaned forward to place a kiss on the youngster's cheek. As she straightened, she asked, "Shall we shake hands on your promise never to scare us to death again?"

Timmy shook her hand in a serious, adult manner, and then Blythe noticed that his eyes had gone past her shoulder to look at something behind her.

Puzzled, she turned and froze.

Cad.

She felt her whole being fill with joy at the sight of him. But then she remembered their altercation, and asked, "How long have you been here?"

"Long enough." He came into the room and approached the bed. "You caused quite a commotion last night, young man."

Timmy's eyes lit up with interest as he surveyed Cad's imposing frame. He didn't get many visitors, and Blythe saw him straighten his shoulders, trying to make a good impression on the stranger.

"I ran away and spent most of the night outside." Pride shone in his face, but then he added more honestly, "I was very brave, but I guess I did cause Miss Bedford a lot of worry. I promised not to do it again." Blythe tried not to smile at the wistfulness in Timmy's tone. He'd rather enjoyed all the attention, but he had to realize that he could get attention in ways that were neither injurious to himself nor disruptive to the whole institute.

"Well, Timmy, you know there's a whole lot of bravery that has nothing to do with having the guts to run away." Cad's eyes met Blythe's as he added, "We men have to be brave enough to admit we're wrong." He looked back at Timmy. "Do you think you're going to be man enough to keep your promise?"

Timmy nodded vigorously, and Blythe saw a smile tilt the corners of Cad's mouth. He patted Timmy's shoulder.

"Timmy, I wasn't here when you explained why

you ran away," Cad said gently.

Timmy hung his head, and played with the bed-clothes. "Miss Bedford used to visit me quite a lot. Lately she didn't come very often, and I thought—I thought—"

"You thought Matthew was right when he said you were going to be sent away." Blythe's eyes filled with tears. She leaned forward and hugged Timmy tightly, and the wetness on her face mixed with the tears on Timmy's. "Oh, Timmy, how could you think that of me? You should know better."

He shrugged, but didn't try to pull away from the embrace. "Well, Mommy and Daddy and Samantha are gone, and sometimes I wonder..."

Blythe kept one arm about his shoulders and raised his chin to look at him. "Your parents' and sister's death was an accident, Timmy. You remember that. An accident. Just like the fact that your shattered hip has caused one leg to be shorter than the other." She hugged him briefly and promised him fervently, "But when you're stronger, we're going to get a surgeon to fix it. Okay?"

Timmy nodded. Then, apparently remembering there was a man in the room, he scrubbed at his face with the back of his hand to remove all traces of tears. Blythe looked in her pocket for a handkerchief, and then remembered she was wearing June's pants and sweater.

A square white cloth appeared in her line of vision, and Blythe accepted it gratefully. She dried her eyes, but resisted the urge to wipe Timmy's face. She left the handkerchief near the boy's pillow, where he'd be sure to see it and have easy access to it.

Cad moved forward and extended his hand. "By the way, my name's Cad Smith."

Timmy shook it happily and answered, "Timmy Singer."

"Would you mind if I stayed and visited with you for a bit, Timmy?"

"Do you know anything about football?" the boy asked eagerly.

"Timmy!" Blythe chided him reproachfully.

"Oh, sorry. I'll be glad if you stay," Timmy amended politely. And then he sat up in bed, excitement lending color to his pale face. "I don't get to talk to too many people. My dad and older sister Sam and me used to watch football on TV all the time. Sometimes we even went to see the games in person. Miss Bedford is nice, but she doesn't know a thing about football."

Cad looked at Blythe, his eyes shining with amusement. "I didn't realize there was anything Ms. Bedford didn't know," he drawled. Then he turned to Timmy and said, "Football's one of my favorite sports. I'd like to discuss some of the games you've seen, and tell you who's on top lately."

"Great!" Timmy said, bouncing on the bed.

"Timmy, don't overdo it," Blythe reproved him. "You have to rest up." To Cad, she said, "You can stay for a few minutes."

When he saw that Timmy was about to protest, Cad said firmly, "I can only stay a little while today, Timmy. But I promise to come back again, when you're allowed to have a visitor for a longer time, and

I'll bring some games along." Looking at Blythe, he added, "I have to go away for a couple of days, but I'll be back."

Their eyes met for a long, silent moment, until Timmy's fidgeting reminded them of their surroundings.

Blythe walked quickly to the door, and said over her shoulder, "Just a few minutes, Timmy. I'll be in later today to see you again for a little while."

She felt confused, disturbed. Cad seemed so comfortable with Timmy—but why would he get involved with a child from the institute? Had he genuinely responded to the boy's neediness, or was he trying to tell her something? Blythe wondered. Without resolving the question, she left them alone.

CHAPTER TWELVE

BLYTHE REALIZED THE extent of her love for Cad
when she got home to an empty house that night.
Loneliness gnawed at her, but she tried to keep herself
from wondering where he was. He had apologized—
albeit indirectly—for his behavior. Gladys had told
her that he'd shown up at the institute yesterday, wanting to see Blythe, and although the secretary had been
surprised, she'd told him to go to the clinic. She hadn't
thought Blythe would mind.

Blythe had reassured Gladys that it was okay, but
had not satisfied her friend's curiosity. Her feelings
were too new, too fragile and uncertain, to be ana-
lyzed, or even brought out in the open.

Now her own curiosity was piqued. About his
whereabouts. About whether he'd found a job. About

whether he'd been able to come to terms with the work she did.

She didn't know if she'd driven him away by her harmless deception. At first she had told herself that Cad was only passing through her life. Knowing his attitudes and beliefs, she'd decided that nothing would be gained from telling him what she did for a living. He might associate her with Alessandra, might suspect her motives.

But he'd been angry with her for holding out on him—very angry. Thinking that she might have lost Cad was painful. But it was equally hard for her to contemplate leaving her job at the institute. She could not abandon those children who needed her so much. They had suffered enough pain, deprivation, and betrayal in their short lives.

She could never add her own desertion to that heavy load they carried. And if a man expected her to give up the children in return for his love, then that man did not love her enough.

As she approached the outer office the following morning, Blythe stopped dead. Justin was seated on the edge of Gladys's desk, his hand cupping her face.

Blythe opened her briefcase, as if looking for something inside, and walked into the room, her high-heeled boots pounding the floor, and her head bent.

"You don't have to be so conspicuously subtle, Blythe," Justin told her as she neared them. "You're going to know soon enough."

Blythe's head rose sharply, and she looked from one happy face to the other.

"Know what?" she asked, smiling.

"That you were right about Gladys. She did have a bit more than professional interest in my mail."

"Hey, wait a minute," Blythe protested, her gaze going worriedly to her friend. "Don't make me sound like a betrayer of confidences—"

"Don't worry, Blythe," Gladys said, laughing and hugging Justin's waist. "I know all you did was give Justin a little nudge in the right direction. I'm grateful to you for expediting matters."

Blythe stepped forward to hug her friends and asked, "Any other news I should be aware of?"

Gladys's smile was mischievous. She reached behind her and said, "There were a couple of messages while you slept late."

"Number one," Blythe said with mock indignation, going along with the teasing, "I did not oversleep. I was checking up on Timmy and Matthew. And number two, I meant what kind of *personal* news might there be that I should be aware of."

"Well," Gladys began, "your parents called. And Nimms's secretary phoned to find out if you were indeed attending the party on Saturday—"

"Gladys!"

"Oh, all right," Gladys said, her face radiant. "Justin and I are engaged, and we'll be throwing a party next month."

"Congratulations! When's the wedding?"

"In the summer," Justin answered. "Gladys wants to be a June bride."

"And I want you to be my bridesmaid," Gladys added. "If you can tear yourself away from work, or from that gorgeous hunk who came in here yesterday like a whirlwind, looking for you..."

"A mystery man?" Justin asked. "This is the first I've heard of it." At Blythe's raised eyebrows, he admitted smilingly, "Okay. You want the truth, don't you? Gladys clued me in to the little she knew."

Blythe developed a sudden urge to attend to her messages. "You say my parents called? And Mrs. Lehman?"

Gladys smiled at Blythe's evasive tactics, but answered dutifully, "Yes, Mrs. Lehman wanted to make sure that you understood the gathering on Saturday is a dress-up affair." Blythe rolled her eyes, and Justin, who knew Blythe's background, snickered. "Your mother and father called; the wire services picked up the story of Timmy's disappearance and carried it nationwide. And, most important, one of the volunteers last night related the incident to a reporter from a local television station. She wants to do a piece on you and the institute."

"Before you say no," Justin said, anticipating Blythe's reaction to appearing on television, "you should consider all the angles. If people know about the plight of some of these children, they might send donations."

Blythe swung her briefcase thoughtfully. "I don't know, Justin," she said, shaking her head. "Lucas went on television once, and it didn't do much good. Remember? Most of the donations we received came from individuals who could barely afford it. The size of each contribution was negligible. And most corporations want to give to a very visible charity, not

a little institute like ours." Then, not wanting to spoil
her friends' happiness, she said, "Let's all go to dinner
tonight to celebrate your engagement, all right? We'll
discuss business tomorrow." She began walking to
the office, still swinging her briefcase, when a thought
occurred to her. "That is, if you two hadn't planned
a more intimate celebration?"

"Tonight will be fine," Justin answered.

Blythe nodded, smiling, then entered her office to
allow Justin some time to say good-bye to Gladys
until they saw each other at lunchtime.

Pushing away the thoughts of Cad that crowded
into her mind, she put a call through to her parents.
She was already anticipating what they would say,
but she wanted to get it over with as soon as possible.

The day passed in a blur. Blythe accomplished a
great deal of work and even handled her telephone
calls to her parents and Mrs. Lehman with aplomb.
Her parents had been predictable, telling her they'd
donate a sizable chunk of money to the institute if she
immediately quit working there. Her answer had been
the usual polite refusal, and she had silently promised
herself that her parents would be her last resort. She'd
accept their help only if the grant was not approved
and she had no other means to save the institute.

Rather than let Gladys return the call of Vincent
Nimms's secretary, Blythe had done it herself, assuring the woman that she did have a suitable dress
and that she would not disgrace herself at the party.
Then she'd sweetly reminded her that she was attending the event for business reasons only and that

she expected Mr. Nimms to honor his commitment this time.

The bright spot of her day had been her talk with Matthew Deylan. He was a very tough, very bitter boy of fourteen who was becoming increasingly hard to control. He'd suffered a double loss the year before: His right arm had been amputated, and the mother he adored had died. His father had died when Matthew was five, so the death of his mother was all the more traumatic for Matthew. He'd become sullen, wild, mean.

But Blythe had been able to get through to the teenager, eventually. Appealing to his sense of fair play and trying to develop his sense of protectiveness, she'd made Matthew understand that Timmy was a victim, like himself. The only difference lay in the fact that Timmy was a small child, and unlike Matthew, he had no way to defend himself yet. If nothing else, Blythe was sure that Matthew could see it was not very sporting of him to pick on someone smaller, younger, and more defenseless.

Matthew had listened thoughtfully this time, and Blythe had added that mental anguish could be more difficult to endure than a physical handicap. But Matthew was old enough, strong enough, and intelligent enough to overcome any difficulties, if only he put his mind to it. And helping, guiding, someone younger, someone who could use an older brother, might take the edge off his own bitterness.

When she'd left, Matthew had been thoughtfully, quietly staring out the window at the softly falling snow.

* * *

"Do you think Nimms will approve the grant?"

"Hey, we agreed not to discuss business tonight, remember?" Blythe told Gladys as they were having dessert that evening.

"I waited until my Tannenbaum Torte," Gladys answered impudently, raising her fork, which was heaped with cake smothered in chocolate and cream. "Dinner's almost over."

"Well, we can wait until tomorrow," Blythe said. "Tonight I want to celebrate your happiness." She raised her wineglass and offered a toast.

Then Justin returned to the attack. "Have you thought about appearing on television?"

Blythe nodded thoughtfully. "Yes, I have thought it over. If nothing comes of Saturday's meeting, then I'll give it serious consideration." She sipped her wine and said, "Now let's get to serious business here. What color have you decided on for the bridal party, Glad? And where will you two live after the wedding?"

Blythe smiled brightly as she listened to Gladys and Justin's plans, but her gaiety was forced. Though she was genuinely happy for her friends, she'd had an exhausting day, considering every angle to solicit funds for the institute. And at the back of her mind was the knowledge that Cad would not be there when she went home that night.

She knew she would find it very hard to fall asleep, not knowing where he was, whether he was well, whether he was thinking of her. She had felt Cad really cared for her, and she didn't think she'd been wrong about him. But his silence of the last couple of days was hard to take, and in her confusion and loneliness, she was beginning to question her judgment.

The following day she visited Timmy after lunch, and began to do a slow burn when the youngster again asked for Cad. She hated having to hedge.

"But do you think he might be here tomorrow maybe? He told me to keep it a secret from all the other children, but he said that he would get us a color television set. He told me I shouldn't have to miss my football games just because the institute has only that old black and white set in the lounge."

Blythe's nails dug into her palms, but she kept her expression casual. "Cad promised you a television set?"

Timmy nodded eagerly. "You won't tell Cad I told, will you? But he's going to get me a color portable, and one apiece for the rest of the kids, too."

Blythe enunciated the words slowly. "He's going to get each of you a color TV set?"

"Yep." Then, knowing something was wrong, but not quite able to put his finger on it, Timmy said somewhat guiltily, "But that's not the only reason I want to see Cad. I mean, I don't want him to visit me just so I can get the TV set. I mean," he explained, obviously trying to be painfully honest, "sure, I want the set, but I really like Cad. He's a lot of fun."

Blythe ruffled his hair. "Oh, Timmy, I know you like Cad. And it's not wrong to want something you were promised. And I know Cad likes you, too," she reassured him. "He must be really busy. He did say he'd be back in a couple of days."

"It's been a couple of days." Timmy's hazel eyes darkened and widened. "You don't suppose anything happened to Cad?"

Blythe felt her heart contract. She hugged Timmy, thinking that at that very moment she could cheerfully have throttled Cad. How dare he do this to a little boy? Cad so easily made a place for himself in a person's heart. And once he was there, it was hard to eradicate him. She could handle false promises, even desertion. But if he'd lied to Timmy . . .

She heard Timmy's tentative, muffled voice. "Miss Bedford? Are you all right? I can't—I can't breathe . . ."

Blythe released the boy immediately. "Oh, Timmy, I'm sorry. Yes, I'm fine. But you're such a huggable kid, I get carried away sometimes."

She saw the pleasure in his eyes before he remembered his tough image and disgustedly ran a hand through the hair she'd just ruffled. "Oh, well, I guess that's okay. My mom used to hug me all the time. And my sister, Sammy, too, except I couldn't stand it when *she* did."

Blythe smiled through her tears, and she surreptitiously brushed them away with her hand. She was glad that Timmy could talk about his family so easily now. When he'd first come to the institute, he had been quiet and withdrawn, and he'd turned rigid at the mere mention of the accident.

Courting the young boy's wrath, she hugged him again, fiercely promising herself that, one way or another, she'd see to it that the institute survived. They had made real progress on several fronts, and many

of the children had begun to feel like part of a big
family. She couldn't allow anyone to hurt these children again.

She left soon afterward, her mind seething. She
was furious at Cad, with his empty promises. Where
in heaven's name was he going to get the money to
pay for one television set, let alone several? And where
was *she* going to get the money to buy Timmy his
portable color set? Then, too, although Timmy hadn't
said anything to the rest of the children, she couldn't
buy a television for just Timmy, either. That would
be blatant favoritism, and although she had a tender
spot for Timmy, Blythe made sure that all the children
received fair, equal treatment.

Where in the hell was she going to get enough
money to provide color sets for the institute?

As she went home that evening, Blythe didn't know
if she was madder at her parents, Vincent Nimms, or
Cad Smith. The first two she was not very surprised
at, but the third she had not credited with such in-
sensitivity and lack of integrity. She wished she could
retain her former impression of Cad. Part of her—a
very large, passionate part—insisted that he was not
capable of such nefarious behavior. But it was hard
to keep defending him and finding excuses for his
actions when he seemed to have vanished without a
trace.

The butler who opened the door for her could have
stepped out of a Basil Rathbone movie. Blythe heaved
a deep sigh and stepped inside the marble foyer of the
mansion.

Guests overflowed the large rooms, spilling into

the foyer. The men were attired in black tie, the women in expensive gowns, which competed with the flash of their jewels as they moved from one conversational island to the other.

This was the kind of life Blythe had run from. She felt somewhat lost among these people. Theirs was a world she'd abandoned, and she felt no nostalgic twinge. Turning to the butler, who was regarding her suspiciously, she asked him to take her to Mr. Nimms right away.

Past one corridor, down some steps, through another hall whose velvet-covered walls bore likenesses of ancestors captured on canvas, Blythe followed the butler to the study where Vincent Nimms was conferring with several other men.

"Mr. Nimms, Ms. Blythe Bedford. She insisted on seeing you right away."

Nimms excused himself from the other men, and told the butler to return to his duties. Blythe nodded to the men who had stood up at her entrance before regally seating herself in the chair Vincent Nimms ushered her to.

"You're saying you won't approve the grant?"

"Exactly that, Ms. Bedford," Nimms said with an apologetic air. "I don't think you've managed the institute properly, and before I approve any monies, I would have to send in a team of experts to find out what you've done to the books."

Blythe twisted her fingers in her lap, crushing the gold material of her gown. But her glance was steady as she met Nimm's cold eyes.

"A team of management consultants will cost you

an arm and a leg," she observed. "You're willing to spend the foundation's money that way rather than give us a grant that you know we desperately need for the children?"

Nimms got up, signaling the end of the discussion. "I don't see anything new in your revised proposal, Ms. Bedford. And as I'm responsible for the disbursement of the Penbrook Foundation's funds, I cannot in good conscience approve anything until I've made a thorough investigation."

Blythe stood up also. Holding herself erect, she smiled coldly. "Please leave your conscience out of this discussion, Mr. Nimms. And you and I both know that I've done an excellent job at the institute—carrying on after the death of my husband."

"Your husband was capable; I'll grant you that. But his death seems to have had an unfortunate effect on your emotional balance. A woman, after all—"

"Mr. Nimms, you're giving me grounds for a civil lawsuit. The fact that I'm a woman has nothing to do with rising costs, the same amount of space, and a steadily increasing number of children. We're doing the best we can, our staff members are doing a first-rate job at lower salaries than they deserve, much lower than they could command elsewhere. We have caring people at the institute, Mr. Nimms. And we have something you wouldn't recognize, because you've probably never encountered it or practiced it: integrity. Please don't bother to show me out."

She walked swiftly to the door, then paused and turned to face her adversary. Her eyes glittering, she told him, "You haven't seen the last of me, Mr. Nimms.

I'm going to fight you, and I'm going to win. *You* are the inept and dishonest one around here. And I will not put up with slander, discrimination, and sheer incompetence."

She tried to contain her fury as she made her way to the front of the house again. Since there were so many guests, she wasn't sure where the butler had put her velvet cape, so she asked one of the maids to locate a maroon cape with golden lining for her.

As she waited in the marble foyer, her eyes ran slowly, uninterestedly, over the crowd, watching familiar rituals. Her mother thrived in this kind of setting, and so did the girls she'd gone to high school with. It was in college that both she and some of her closest friends had become completely disillusioned with the goldfish-bowl life they led. And then she'd met Lucas.

Lucas.

The name would always bring inner joy to her. They had both grown together, learned from each other. They'd loved well.

On the heels of that came another memory. More recent, more potent. And very painful.

So when she saw a golden head topping broad shoulders exquisitely contained in a dark tuxedo, Blythe knew she was imagining things. A mirage inspired by loneliness, by frustration, by a sense of desperation.

She shook herself out of her somber mood, telling herself Nimms would not win, when the head turned and her heart stopped.

Cad. But it couldn't be. The head turned another

fraction of an inch, and golden-green eyes were rapidly looking her over, then returning to her face, locking with her own wide blue eyes.

Blythe saw recognition in those clear depths. Then shock. Then worry.

Then guilt.

Fury rose in her throat, and she looked desperately about her. She saw the maid heading for her with her cape at the same moment that Cad quickly advanced toward her.

Blythe snatched the cape from the maid, thanked her hurriedly, and huddled in its satin lining as she headed blindly for the door. She felt numb, and she was thankful for her lack of emotion, because Cad's betrayal ran so deep that to feel its impact would, she knew, be devastating.

She heard Cad call her name, and his image burned itself into her mind: his face pale underneath the tan; his wild, wavy hair combed into submission; his attire and stance that of a man accustomed to these gatherings. His posture bespoke breeding, poise. And infinite wealth.

The butler opened the door for her, bowing his head in stiff correctness. Blythe felt like laughing. There were some things that had remained the same for centuries. There was, after all, something to be said for tradition, she thought as her gold sandals flew down the front steps.

Her velvet cape floating behind her, her hood coming off to allow the wind to have its way with her thick coronet, Blythe ran to her car. She tried the engine, and groaned when its age and unreliability

caused it to fail her when she most needed it. Cursing,
she pushed a damp tendril of red-gold hair away from
her face. Desperately turning the key again, she felt
her heart sink. The cold weather had taken its toll on
the old car. And it would not start tonight without the
help of a mechanic.

"Blythe!"

She turned at the sound and tried to lock the door
against Cad. But he was already opening it and pulling
her from the car.

"Dammit, Cad! Let me go!"

"After we've talked." Ignoring her struggles, he
carried her to a nineteenth-century-style carriage that
stood nearby. He climbed in, sitting her on his lap.

"Drive around the grounds, please," he told the
driver.

Seeing that she could not break free, Blythe desisted in her struggles. When Cad lowered his head,
she turned hers away. She wouldn't stoop to the in-
dignity of a quarrel in her long gown in a carriage in
freezing weather within hearing of a circumspect driver.
But she would never feel the same about Cad Smith.

But Cad didn't try to kiss her. Instead, he whispered the words that she had longed to hear before he
left: "I love you." But now those words didn't have
the same meaning or impact they would have had if
he'd uttered them when she still knew him as a ski
bum. Too late, she thought.

She could feel Cad's gaze boring into the top of
her head. She could sense him waiting for her reply,
but she stubbornly refused him any sort of response.

Cad tenderly pulled the hood of the cape up over

her head, and said softly, "It's true, Blythe. I do love
you. I didn't realize how strongly I felt when I left
Indian Cove and followed you here. But any doubts
I might have had disappeared once we lived together."
Blythe stiffened, not wanting him to discuss anything
so intimate in the presence of the driver. But he continued on a different tack. "Blythe, I made an ass of
myself the night of Timmy's disappearance. That's
why I tried to make amends by hiring those two detectives. I wanted—"

Blythe turned to face him in the diffuse light of
the moon. "How easy everything is for you, Cad. Just
snap your fingers, and somebody else does your work.
It would have been too much for you to help out,
wouldn't it?"

"Blythe—"

Her bitterness mounted. "And what about those
television sets? Those children need more than color
TV sets, Cad. Sure it would be nice if they had them,
but that's a luxury. They need sound limbs and bodies
and minds first, and a good education. And people
who care for them—"

"Mr. Penbrook-Smith." The driver coughed dis-
creetly, cutting into Blythe's angry tirade. "It is freezing, sir, and you don't have an overcoat. May I point
out that perhaps you and the young lady could continue your discussion inside the house?"

Only one thing registered for Blythe.

"Did he call you *Penbrook*-Smith?"

Cad nodded. "I didn't really lie to you. Just omitted
part of my name, which is quite cumbersome. Cadwallader Penbrook-Smith IV."

Blythe felt as if her insides were on fire. Not only had Cad deceived her about his wealth, but also about his very identity. He was the head of the Penbrook Foundation! Nimms had refused her the grant, but Nimms was only an underling. The final decision rested with Cad.

"You're the head of the Penbrook Foundation," she said tonelessly.

He nodded. "That's right. My financial interests are far-flung, and I also handle the financial affairs of my parents, my older brother, Eugene, and my younger sister, Amelia." Then, at her stricken look, he locked his arms tightly about her. "I'm sorry, Sky Eyes. I didn't make the connection because you didn't tell me where you worked. You're the one whose grant Nimms said we should refuse." He squeezed her waist reassuringly. "Don't worry about it. I'll look into this one personally. I'm not sure why Nimms is so set against giving you those funds, but I'll get the whole matter cleared up. And you'll get the grant. You don't have to worry about that."

"Nimms says I'm incompetent. That man gets his kicks out of acting like God. But I don't place all the blame on him. You should know what kind of people are handling your foundation funds. But you're obviously too busy playing the rich playboy, dazzling women with your charm, instead of investigating your holdings, or at least personally supervising the people to whom you delegated authority." Cad's eyes darkened at her accusations, and she added, "I despise your policy—and those of many wealthy people I've met, including my own parents, who give only to reduce their income taxes." Pushing at his chest, trying to get away from him, she saw that they had almost reached the white-columned facade of the building. "You condemned Alessandra, but you're not better than she was." Jumping from his lap, she leaped out of the carriage before he was able to stop her. As she ran away, she yelled, "And I'm not for sale, Cad Penbrook-Smith."

Some taxis were delivering late arrivals, and Blythe hailed one that was leaving the circular driveway, jumping into it before a stunned Cad could reach her.

CHAPTER THIRTEEN

"BLYTHE, MR. PENBROOK-SMITH—"

"Glad, I told you I don't even want to hear that odious man's name. Get him off the phone, and quickly, please." The gall of the man! He'd called her all day yesterday, and though Gladys had transmitted the message that Blythe wouldn't talk to him, Cad had kept up the phone calls all morning. Gladys had reported that he was calling every half-hour, and Blythe had told the secretary not even to inform her anymore when he called.

"But Blythe—"

"Glad, just get rid of him!"

A male voice spoke into the intercom. "I'm afraid she can't. I'm bigger than she is, and I won't go peaceably."

Blythe stared at the device on her desk as if it had suddenly turned into a Medusa. Then, outraged, she picked up her jacket from the back of her chair and pulled it on as she walked to the door and flung it open.

"What the hell do you think you're—" Her words fizzled out as she saw the boxes surrounding Gladys's desk. Television sets.

She spotted Cad in the middle of the cartons, and she realized that the physical attraction was still there. But she told herself that Cad was a very handsome man—almost irresistible in his dark suit and lemon-yellow silk shirt—and her hormones had always been healthy. The important thing, she reminded herself, was that she no longer felt any deeper emotion for Cad.

"Please take those things out of here. We don't need your largesse."

"Is that the children talking, or a very proud Blythe Bedford?"

"You know we need a lot of things more than we need those TV sets—"

"And you're getting whatever you need. Just ask, and ye shall receive."

Gladys, who had stayed in the background, her eyes going from one to the other as if she were watching a Ping-Pong match, jumped in, "Why, that's wonderful, Blythe! Now we can even consider all those expansions that were only dreams before!"

"Don't dream, please, Glad. This gentleman doesn't mean what he says."

Gladys looked confused. "You mean he's not the

head of the Penbrook Foundation? Or has the foundation been dissolved?"

"I mean that Vincent Nimms rejected our petition for the grant. He didn't approve of my proposal."

"And he's been fired," Cad put in quietly. "You were right, Sky Eyes. I should have paid closer attention to the people who work for me. Rest assured that in the future I'll screen people for key positions very closely."

"I don't really care what you do in the future, Cad," Blythe told him frostily. She pointed to the television sets. "Just get those out of the building."

Cad moved toward her. "Are you going to deny the children out of your own capriciousness, Blythe? I thought they meant more than that to you."

Her eyes sent daggers at him, but he withstood them. "That's a cheap shot, Cad," she said in a low voice. "Even for you."

He winced but held her gaze. "Blythe, I know you're hurting right now. And I don't blame you for lashing out at me."

Blythe opened her mouth to interrupt him, not wanting Gladys to hear any of this, not wanting any memories recalled. But he forestalled her. "Please, let me finish." She closed her mouth, and her mind. There really was nothing he could say to excuse his deception.

"The money's already on its way to you," he said. "You'll find it's more than you requested from Nimms, and it's yours to use as you see fit. I expect to be kept notified of your plans until I find a replacement for Nimms, but you won't be bogged down with reports.

Nor will you have to account for every penny. I will only want to be advised of major expenditures. And you will, of course, be free to expand your staff and raise the salaries of those who deserve more money."

He paused, waiting for an answer from Blythe. She remained unyielding. "Is that all?"

He sighed. "Yes, that's all. For now. Except that I'd like to talk to you as soon as you're able to forgive me."

"Don't hold your breath," Blythe told him. Then, as he was about to leave, she called him back. "Cad!"

She saw a light of hope shine in the golden-green eyes, but it died a quick death as he saw her expression hadn't changed. "Timmy's been asking for you. You may as well give him his TV personally. For some reason, he took a liking to you, and I'm sure he'll be glad to see you."

He smiled at her reluctant tone, a smile that started slowly and built until it illuminated his whole face, catching her in the web of its radiance. "I know that must have been hard for you. And thanks, I will. I like Timmy, and if you don't mind, I'd like to get to know the other children, too."

She made a sweeping motion with her hand. "Be my guest. It's your money."

She saw the smile disappear from Cad's face and out of the corner of her eye caught Gladys's disapproving expression. But she couldn't so easily forget the loneliness she'd felt when Cad had disappeared from her life, or the pain that had ripped her apart when she'd seen him in that mansion, blending right in with the other wealthy people of that world. He'd belonged in it, and had even seemed to be enjoying it. And the man—the lover—she'd known and loved as Cad Smith had vanished before her eyes like a mirage before a wanderer dying of thirst. Perhaps Cad had always been that way, and she'd given him the qualities she'd desired.

But as she turned her back on the television sets and on Cad, she told herself that if indeed she had created a mirage, she hadn't done so alone. Cad had helped, acting like a chameleon to fit the image he knew she'd prefer.

And that betrayal hurt worst of all.

The days passed slowly.

Despite the increased revenue, and the new solvency that allowed them to put into operation plans they'd only dreamed of before, Blythe found that the days went by with excruciating slowness. She had a lot of work, and she still enjoyed it.

But the winter proved cruel and unrelenting. And she hated going home at night.

Valentine's Day came and went, and so did Justin's and Gladys's engagement party. Blythe attended it and was happy for her friends, but she left early, sure that she wouldn't be missed in the large, happy crowd.

But she was wrong. She'd only just arrived home when the phone rang, and a worried Gladys asked her if she was all right. After assuring Gladys that, yes, everything was just fine, that she had a slight headache and would call her tomorrow to find out how the party went, Blythe hung up and sat in the dark for a while, watching the snow that was once again turning their world into a white wonderland.

But even the snow had lost some of its magical
appeal. Disgusted with herself, Blythe got up, put on
some ABBA tapes, and decided to give the apartment
an early spring cleaning.

When she came to the plants that Cad had resus-
citated from a moribund state in his short stay, but
that were now again undernourished and clawing at
the window as if seeking escape, Blythe felt the ice
of winter begin to thaw in her. She remembered the
few days that Cad had spent in the apartment—they
were some of the best hours in her entire life. He'd
made her come alive, with his special touch, and his
special humor, and his special tenderness.

Could she have been wrong to turn against him?
True, there was the matter of his deception. Yet, she'd
also deceived him. And for basically the same reasons.

He'd told her he'd be there when she was ready to
forgive him. It was a bit too soon yet. She had a lot
of things to work out in her mind.

But she had to know if what she'd felt for Cad *was*
only a mirage. If it had been a double deception on
their parts. If it had been self-deception.

Being apart for a while longer would be hard for
her. But easier in the long run. They'd hurt each other,
and it was best to let the wounds heal.

In another month, though . . .

In another month, there would be spring thaws . . .

Four weeks later Blythe returned to Indian Cove.
Only this time she was not seeking solitude, or a
sanctuary from hurt.

This time she was looking for someone.

She registered quickly and asked the clerk if Mr. Smith had already arrived. The clerk looked at her with a puzzled frown. "Mr. Smith? Oh, Mr. Penbrook-Smith." His brow cleared. "No, I haven't seen him yet, but then, I've only been on duty for a couple of hours. And Mr. Penbrook-Smith likes to travel incognito. He arrives and departs with little notice. He prefers it that way. He doesn't like to be fussed over."

Blythe smiled. How unobservant of her not have noticed that Cad felt so at home at the resort. He'd even told her he owned it. Yet, she hadn't believed him.

"Thank you," she told the clerk with a smile so radiant that he blinked.

All of a sudden, she knew Cad was here. She could sense it. And she also knew exactly where he was.

Going upstairs to her room, she quickly changed and rented a snowmobile. She drove too fast, and the vehicle made too much noise for her to catch sight of deer or other wild animals.

And then she was at their spot. The waterfall, which still had patches of ice clinging tenaciously to the gray stone, catching the little light that filtered through the trees and reflecting it back with diamondlike brilliance.

She walked slowly toward the ice-and-water sculpture, breathing deeply of the fresh, biting air, heavy with the promise of trees and flowers that would soon begin to return to life as the ground and the forest renewed themselves.

She sensed his presence. She didn't hear him approach, but she could tell he was there.

She turned, and his arms closed about her.

"I wasn't sure you'd come," Cad said, his lips buried in the hair she'd left unbound to trail like a flaming river down her back.

She looked up at him, at the golden-green eyes that reflected all his moods, and that had first mirrored his feelings for her. "How could you doubt it? I did say I'd meet you here in the spring."

He chuckled, and the sound chased chills up her spine. "That was a lifetime ago, when you still thought I was Cad Smith. Before I'd hurt you with my stupid deception."

She hugged him fiercely and delivered a hard kiss.

"Yes, you did hurt me. But I should have realized you were trying to tell me something when I was here. I guess once I discovered your charade, I was so scared you belonged to the old world I'd left behind that I ignored any clues you planted in my way."

He kissed the tip of her nose and told her, "And I was so afraid you would thoroughly despise Cadwallader Penbrook-Smith IV—which you ended up doing—that I continued the charade past the time I told myself I would end it." He kissed her again, deeply, devouringly, and asked, "Will you forgive me?"

She nodded and buried her face in his neck. "I love you." When his arms closed convulsively about her, she looked up and smiled at him. "I told you before, when we first made love, but you didn't hear me."

"If I had, I'd have told you who I was right away.

But just as I wasn't sure about my feelings at first, I was even more unsure about yours."

She brought his head down for a kiss, and told him against his mouth, "You never have to be uncertain again."

CHAPTER FOURTEEN

"WON'T YOUR PARENTS be upset that you got married without inviting them?"

Blythe shrugged, unconcerned. They were spending their wedding night in Cad's suite at Indian Cove, awaiting the procession of light that was soon to descend on the hill visible from the wall-sized French windows.

"I'll let my parents know about my marriage after the honeymoon. They'll be happy to know I've married someone suitable this time, but my mother would have tried to force a formal wedding. All they're interested in is my returning to the fold to carry on their traditions. They've got Harlan to work on now; he surprised us all by getting engaged." She snuggled contentedly against Cad and brushed her fingers over his forehead, down his nose, and over his cheeks, which had begun to get stubbly. "We'll create our own traditions."

He trapped one of her fingers inside his mouth and sucked it so imaginatively that Blythe's breathing quickened. He spoke around it. "What about your friends Gladys and Justin? You cheated them out of attending your wedding."

Blythe rose on her elbows to lean her upper torso on Cad's. The room was pleasantly cool, and she felt engulfed by his heat. "Glad will forgive me. We'll be attending her wedding in June, and I know she'll wish us happy. Justin, too."

Cad left her a moment to add some wood to the fireplace, which was flanked by windows. "I didn't realize I'd find such a good use for this oversized room one day. But it sure does ensure privacy." He stoked the fire, then set the poker down. "We could stay here until summer. No one will miss us."

Blythe laughed. "No? I can think of a few people who will. And I'm sure your stockholders would have something to say about your disappearance."

Cad came back to her side and held out a hand to her. "Let's go to the window. I've just seen the first torch."

Blythe got up and he stood behind her as they watched the flames flickering against the iridescent snow and the ebony sky. "Blythe, I'm sorry I pulled that disappearing act on you after Timmy ran away. I was trying to get my head together, and I had a board meeting the following afternoon and had to fly to the East Coast after that. It won't happen again."

She took her eyes away from the sinuous, scintillating light procession and twisted her head to kiss him. "It'd better not." A memory tugged at her mind, and she asked, "Cad, did you help search for Timmy the night he disappeared? It seems to me I saw you, but I wanted to have you there so badly that I later thought I'd imagined it."

He laced his arms about her waist and dropped a kiss on her upturned chin. "I'll never tell."

"You *were* there, weren't you?" she said with sudden conviction. "Oh, I'm sorry, Cad." She covered his hands with hers and caressed them. "After what I said to you—"

"No more than what I said to myself for carrying on that idiotic deception for so long. We could have been married a long time before this."

She grew thoughtful, and stroked the wiry strength of his inner wrists. "I don't know, Cad. I had to have my time for mourning first, and then, when I met you, I had to become ready to accept the presence of another man in my life." She brought one of her hands to his face and said, "Besides, I needed time to get to know Cad Smith, the ski bum. He's the best part of you, Cad. And he belongs to just the two of us. He's the one I fell in love with, and I'll always know he's there, even when you're playing the role of tycoon."

He cupped her face and looked deeply into her eyes. "Are you sure you don't mind my being wealthy, Blythe? My having to travel?"

She smiled up at him, serene. "I don't mind your wealth, because you've never acted like the other wealthy men I knew. Money is just a tool for you; your identity doesn't depend on it. I like the things we'll be able to do with it, especially at the institute. And when I turn thirty, I'll come into some money of my own." She turned to look at the winding procession, the twinkling of lights seeming to celebrate this very special night. "And as for your traveling, I'll have my work to keep me busy. I'll never feel lonely, because I know you'll be coming back shortly."

"And you won't mind heading my new division for charitable projects? Or commuting to Eau Claire on weekends?" Cad had explained that his brother, Eugene, named after their maternal grandfather, lived in St. Paul, and his sister, Amelia, in another family home in Milwaukee, where she'd returned to get her master's degree. Cad lived in Eau Claire, in what had been his parents' mansion until they retired to one of the Seychelles.

She rubbed the back of her head against his chest, letting her pliant curves mold themselves to his angular frame. "I think it's a terrific idea. I'll always work at the institute, but once I hire more staff, I'll be able to take on other things. And there are so many things we can do, Cad, for Timmy and many other children."

She felt his reverent kiss on her hair before he brought her around and bent his head, slowly, languorously, and kissed her tenderly on the lips, their mouths communicating on a deep, wordless level that promised, reassured, loved, confided, treasured.

Cad kept their mouths joined as he dropped to his knees, bringing her down with him. Quickly, deftly, he disposed of their clothes and then dug his hands into her silken hair, which tumbled into disarray.

Her head fell back, exposing the long, ivory curve of her throat, and he paid homage to it, his kisses preparing her for the tumult awaiting them. His hands lazily circled, drawing arcs on her responsive flesh, until she was shivering with desire and rested her damp forehead against his chest.

Kissing the soft skin that sheathed layers of firm, taut muscle, she began a sensual counterattack of her own. But when he simultaneously cupped her breast and the delta of her femininity, she gasped, collapsing against him in sensual lethargy.

Cad kneaded her breast, weighing it, lifting it, rubbing his thumb over the pouting nipple, before exploring its twin. His other hand stroked and pressed, scratching lightly from her navel downward and upward again, before entering the scorching, slick softness, which was readied for him.

Blythe convulsed against him at his erotic searching, and her own hands lowered to his buttocks to pull him closer. Cad groaned, sliding his finger on the highly charged button that guarded her moist portal. His lips went to her mouth to savor the moan that greeted his searing friction.

Then he was pushing her backward, his hot, engorged manhood replacing his seeking hand, and Blythe had a last view of the sparkling procession down the steep hill. Then sizzling lights were reflected against her closed eyelids when Cad lifted her hips and slid inside. She felt herself expand against his pulsating length, the empty ache filled as he plunged inside, withdrew, then thrust inside even deeper, his hands guiding her hips, his flesh making her throb inside and out.

The sensation was so intense that when he buried his face in her throat in his own agonized pleasure, she opened her mouth and sucked on his salty skin. He shuddered, then thrust deeper, his quickening, smooth strokes stretching her and filling her to the bursting point.

Their hands traveled each other's body, seeking desperate release from the overwhelming pressure, and they pressed together, attempting to remove all physical barriers while cementing their spirits. When Cad felt the trembling start deep within her, spreading and diffusing until her legs, which were curled about his waist, began to shiver, he delved savagely into her body, remaining imbedded in her snug, moist warmth until she rode out her explosion of sensation and feeling. He remained locked within her, receiving and absorbing the tremulous aftershocks, and when she subsided beneath him, he began to move against her once more, exploring her honeyed depths with ever-increasing speed, until his frenzied tempo ended in one deep, ferocious stroke and a groan of ecstasy that reverberated through her sensitized nerve synapses.

They lay fused for a long moment, neither wanting to sever the precious union. Finally, Cad's heaving breath quieted, and his heartbeat steadied against her flesh.

Lifting himself on his elbows, he looked down at her in the light of the flickering fire. "We've wasted too much time. A lifetime with you won't be enough."

Blythe's eyes sparkled with a wet glitter, and she tightened her arms about his neck, bringing his head down for a sweet, tender kiss. "I love you," she told him, her body writhing and flexing beneath his once more, her skin hungry for his touch.

Their lips joined in another kiss, and then Cad's hands lowered to her rounded derriere, kneading the twin mounds with seductive expertise. "What do you say we go for a midnight swim?"

She shook her head. Perhaps sensual fumes had fogged her hearing. "Did I hear right? A midnight swim?"

He nodded, his golden-green eyes sparkling in the semigloom. "It *is* almost midnight."

"It's not the time I'm concerned about, but the weather. It may be spring, but northern Wisconsin doesn't particularly care about the calendar. It's freezing out there."

"But think of how we can warm each other up," Cad tempted her.

"We'll catch pneumonia," Blythe protested, weakening under the expert licking of his tongue on her breast.

"Not if we make it a quick dip," he assured her against her moisture-sheened skin.

"If I catch a cold, or worse—"

"You'll get to stay in bed, and I'll keep you company. But it won't happen. We'll have our own methods of keeping warm."

As Cad lifted her to her feet, Blythe said with less than total conviction, "I'm game if you are."

* * *

Forty minutes later, Blythe moaned as Cad entered her, his strong thrusts making her burn inside and out.

"Are you cold?" he asked, his talented hands finding and pleasuring those spots that made her quiver under his touch.

Blythe's arms closed convulsively about his neck, and her legs rubbed against his before wrapping about his waist. "You devil, you know I'm not." She put her hand between their bodies and raked her nails along his lightly matted chest and the soft thicket covering his groin before venturing lower and applying subtle pressure.

A groan escaped Cad's lips and his whole body shuddered.

"Are you cold, darling?" Blythe asked, her eyes wide and laughing.

Cad's fingers dug into her buttocks, and he brought her hips even closer with a masterful sweep of his hands.

"You make me shiver with love and sensation, Sky Eyes. But don't worry, we'll both be beyond cold and sensation soon."

And he suited action to words.

WONDERFUL ROMANCE NEWS!

Do you know about the exciting SECOND CHANCE AT LOVE/TO HAVE AND TO HOLD newsletter? Are you on our *free* mailing list? If reading all about your favorite authors, getting sneak previews of their latest releases, and being filled in on all the latest happenings and events in the romance world sound good to you, then you'll love our SECOND CHANCE AT LOVE and TO HAVE AND TO HOLD Romance News.

If you'd like to be added to our mailing list, just fill out the coupon below and send it in…and we'll send you your *free* newsletter every three months — hot off the press.

☐ *Yes, I would like to receive your free SECOND CHANCE AT LOVE/TO HAVE AND TO HOLD newsletter.*

Name _____

Address _____

City _____ **State/Zip** _____

Please return this coupon to:

Berkley Publishing
200 Madison Avenue, New York, New York 10016
Att: Rebecca Kaufman

74

HERE'S WHAT READERS
ARE SAYING ABOUT

Second Chance at Love®

"I think your books are great. I love to read them, as does my family."
— *P. C., Milford, MA**

"Your books are some of the best romances I've read."
— *M. B., Zeeland, MI**

"SECOND CHANCE AT LOVE is my favorite line of romance novels."
— *L. B., Springfield, VA**

"I think SECOND CHANCE AT LOVE books are terrific. I married my 'Second Chance' over 15 years ago. I truly believe love is lovelier the second time around!"
— *P. P., Houston, TX**

"I enjoy your books tremendously."
— *I. S., Bayonne, NJ**

"I love your books and read them all the time. Keep them coming—they're just great."
— *G. L., Brookfield, CT**

"SECOND CHANCE AT LOVE books are definitely the best!"
— *D. P., Wabash, IN**

*Name and address available upon request

Second Chance at Love.

____07822-0 **WANTON WAYS #206** Katherine Granger
____07823-9 **A TEMPTING MAGIC #207** Judith Yates
____07956-1 **HEART IN HIDING #208** Francine Rivers
____07957-X **DREAMS OF GOLD AND AMBER #209** Robin Lynn
____07958-8 **TOUCH OF MOONLIGHT #210** Liz Grady
____07959-6 **ONE MORE TOMORROW #211** Aimée Duvall
____07960-X **SILKEN LONGINGS #212** Sharon Francis
____07961-8 **BLACK LACE AND PEARLS #213** Elissa Curry
____08070-5 **SWEET SPLENDOR #214** Diana Mars
____08071-3 **BREAKFAST WITH TIFFANY #215** Kate Nevins
____08072-1 **PILLOW TALK #216** Lee Williams
____08073-X **WINNING WAYS #217** Christina Dair
____08074-8 **RULES OF THE GAME #218** Nicola Andrews
____08075-6 **ENCORE #219** Carole Buck
____08115-9 **SILVER AND SPICE #220** Jeanne Grant
____08116-7 **WILDCATTER'S KISS #221** Kelly Adams
____08117-5 **MADE IN HEAVEN #222** Linda Raye
____08118-3 **MYSTIQUE #223** Ann Cristy
____08119-1 **BEWITCHED #224** Linda Barlow
____08120-5 **SUDDENLY THE MAGIC #225** Karen Keast
____08200-7 **SLIGHTLY SCANDALOUS #226** Jan Mathews
____08201-5 **DATING GAMES #227** Elissa Curry
____08202-3 **VINTAGE MOMENTS #228** Sharon Francis
____08203-1 **IMPASSIONED PRETENDER #229** Betsy Osborne
____08204-X **FOR LOVE OR MONEY #230** Dana Daniels
____08205-8 **KISS ME ONCE AGAIN #231** Claudia Bishop
____08206-6 **HEARTS AT RISK #232** Liz Grady
____08207-4 **SEAFLAME #233** Sarah Crewe
____08208-2 **SWEET DECEPTION #234** Diana Mars
____08209-0 **IT HAD TO BE YOU #235** Claudia Bishop
____08210-4 **STARS IN HER EYES #236** Judith Yates
____08211-2 **THIS SIDE OF PARADISE #237** Cinda Richards

All of the above titles are $1.95
Prices may be slightly higher in Canada.